To Writers With Love

To Writers With Love

On Writing Romantic Novels

MARY WIBBERLEY

For Renée, with best
wishes for your success
in writing

Mary Wibberley

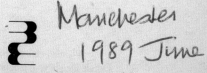

Manchester
1989 June

BUCHAN & ENRIGHT, PUBLISHERS
LONDON

First published in 1985, reprinted 1986, by
Buchan & Enright, Publishers, Limited,
53 Fleet Street, London EC4Y 1BE

British Library Cataloguing in Publication Data

Wibberley, Mary
   To writers with love : on writing romantic
   novels.
   1. Love stories — Authorship
   I. Title
   808.3'85   PN3377.5.L68

   ISBN 0-907675-78-6

Photoset in North Wales by
Derek Doyle & Associates, Mold, Clwyd
Printed and bound by
The Guernsey Press Co. Ltd., Guernsey, Channel Islands

For
Derek, Judith, David
and my super mum,
with love

Contents

Acknowledgements

My thanks to all those who have helped along the way. To my writer friends at Swanwick and Scarborough who answered my questionnaire, and also those I interviewed: Aileen Armitage, Jane Donnelly, Catherine Fellows, Julia Fitzgerald, Margery Hilton, Eileen Jackson, Alanna Knight, Jean Saunders, Anne Thomas and Sheila Walsh. Thanks also to Dr Peter H. Mann, for telling me all I wanted to know about the readership of romantic novels. And thanks to Colin Kilpatrick for advice and encouragement on the practical side. And to Rita Whitelaw for deciphering my handwriting, as she has often done in the past, and typing it out.

Finally my grateful thanks to all those other writers whose words of wit and wisdom I have quoted, and whose opening sentences I have so enjoyed in their books.

If I've missed anyone, humble apologies. I'll give you a free copy.

Introduction

WHEN I put down my pen for the last time and go to that Great Writer's Workshop in the Sky, my first task will be to ensure that there are unlimited supplies of paper (narrow feint, no margins, A4 size), my second that there are a few thousand pens (Bic crystal, black, medium point). If there aren't, I'm not staying.

I was born writing. No, that's an exaggeration. I waited a few months, but as soon as I discovered that crayons made interesting marks on paper, I was away. Unfortunately, in the wrong direction. I am left-handed, and had what the doctor informed my bewildered parents were mirror-eyes. I saw all the print the wrong way round, and in those first stumbling forays into story writing, my efforts could only be read by being held up to a mirror. As I was always writing notes to my family, they spent quite a lot of time squinting into looking-glasses, which puzzled me. I could read them, why couldn't they?

The doctor had said the condition would fade, and it did, fortunately well before I was six, so that when I went hot-foot to the library to join, my name and address were fairly neatly printed in the correct manner. And those two library tickets were the passport to the magic world of books, my kind of books – Andrew Lang's fairy stories, those of the Brothers Grimm, Richmal Crompton's William books, Enid Blyton's adventure stories, and all the other old favourites.

And I also wrote. Stories, plays, poems, articles, all profusely illustrated, hundreds of them came pouring out. I persuaded my friends to act in the plays, and can remember writing programmes, lavishly coloured with pink borders (shades of what was to come?) and the optimistic price: 'one penny'. I'm not sure if anyone ever paid, come to think of it, but it didn't matter. The play was the thing that counted. I was definitely a juvenile ham, even at seven.

Then at the age of thirty, after some minor published successes (children's stories in newspapers, humorous articles on local radio), I sat down one day to think. What had I done with my life? My first child, Judith, was seven months old, and I'd just finished breast-feeding her and had got my mind back after months of being totally bovine, drifting around in an aura of gripe water, nappies and little bootees, incapable of even reading (except mother-and-baby magazines of course) let alone actually writing. All right, this was it. I was going to write a book. Not only was I going to write and complete it (yes, I'd done several, but never quite finished them!) but I was going to get it published.

I found a notebook, and wrote in it in bold block capitals: '**I AM GOING TO WRITE A BOOK AND GET IT PUBLISHED.**' Somehow, that set the seal on it. It became a challenge, a fact waiting to be accomplished. Of course, it took me seven years and seven books before I did, but, fortunately for my iron resolve, I didn't know that at the time. As it was virtually impossible to find a spare moment during the day, I waited until Judith was safely tucked up after her last feed, and Derek, my husband, had gone to bed, and, at about eleven-thirty, I sat down and began to write the book. It took me eight weeks, writing for about three or four hours every night until I crawled up to bed exhausted.

I paid someone to type it because at that time I was absolutely hopeless with a typewriter, and went around telling everyone that I had written a book (a fatal mistake), and sent it off to a publisher, I forget which one, probably Collins. And then I waited complacently for it to be published. Only it wasn't. What I should have done – and what I'm advising you to do – was to have started the next book. It makes the waiting time pass that much more quickly, and because you haven't suffered the blow of rejection, you still have bags of confidence. So that's your first lesson. Immediately you have sent off your first typescript, sit down and begin the next opus. It will occupy your mind wonderfully and save you biting your nails as you wonder what is happening to your precious first-born.

It took me three rejections before I cottoned on to this idea, so that while typescripts were hurtling back and forth, courtesy of Her Majesty's Post Office, I was already engaged on number four. It didn't stop me having a little cry of course, when the inevitable happened, but it did soften the blow somewhat.

I wasn't aware that I was writing romantic novels. As far as I was concerned I was writing what I enjoyed, books full of incident, sometimes mystery, one with kidnapping and stolen diamonds hidden in a doll, another with Russian spies – *but*, and this again I didn't notice until a friend who had bravely read all the books remarked on it – they all had a strong thread of romance in, and they all had rather dishy heroes.

It was about this time, 1970, that several coincidences happened that gave new purpose to my writing, and made me concentrate on one publisher to the exclusion of all others. First, I had heard of, and joined, the Romantic Novelists' Association; secondly, I went for the first time to the Writers' Summer School in Derbyshire; and thirdly, one day, in a Manchester bookshop, buying books, I was given a copy of a free magazine called *Book News*. Inside was an article headed: 'Love is all. A Survey of Women's Fiction'. It was a light-hearted summary of all kinds of novels written by women, from Jane Austen to Barbara Cartland. It also had an interview with Alan Boon, of which one sentence caught my attention and held it, and I kept returning to it, again and again. This is the sentence: 'One surprising fact to emerge is that there is such a shortage of writers that Mills & Boon are now reprinting titles that first saw the light of day in the thirties.' It's easy to say in retrospect that that sentence changed my life – but it did. I found my old notebook of five years previously and updated the promise I had made to myself. It now read: '**I AM GOING TO WRITE A BOOK AND GET IT PUBLISHED BY MILLS AND BOON.**' Four words added, that was all, but it was enough.

I then met Clare Bretton-Smith (who wrote at that time for Mills & Boon under the pseudonym of Hilary Wilde), at the writers' conference, and she was extremely kind and helpful and gave me some marvellous advice. And Helen MacGregor, the reader for the RNA, sent me a crit of one of my manuscripts which said, 'This is potential Mills & Boon material.' That was it. The following months saw me carrying home truckloads of all the M & B's I could get my hands on, from library, bookshops, second-hand markets stalls, and corner-shop library shelves (alas, too few of those). And I read, studied and analysed several hundred of them, until I was steeped in the atmosphere of the books, until I was eating, sleeping, breathing Mills & Boon, in between looking after a growing family. (I now had a son, David.)

I then wrote two more, which went to M & B via the RNA — *and were rejected*. All, as had the others been, with pleasant letters — 'not quite on our wavelength', etcetera. But this time was I daunted? You bet your life I wasn't. I'm proud to say I didn't even cry because I was by now absolutely determined that my next book would be accepted by them, and if it wasn't, I had decided to submit more books under different names, using friends' addresses in case the publishers were fed up with seeing the old familiar words: 'By Mary Wibberley' on typescripts and didn't bother to read them properly. Nothing, but nothing, was going to stop me, I decided. I would bombard them with books until they capitulated.

It wasn't necessary. One day I sat down and looked over the very first book I had ever written, at the age of sixteen, pre-marriage, pre-children, pre-even thinking about anything I had written being considered publishable. I wrote entirely for my own pleasure at that time, simply because I was and always had been, a compulsive writer. Exercise books had only ever existed for me to write stories in, as far as I was concerned, which probably explains why I got such abysmal marks for every subject except English and Art at school.

This sixteen-year-old's efforts (I had never even given it a title) had been about a family feud between the MacBains and the Mackays, set in the Highlands of Scotland, a part of the world where I had spent many happy holidays with my aunt and uncle. The book had been written in the form of a diary by Alison MacKay, the heroine, with whom I identified totally. I enjoyed re-reading it very much. So much so that I knew I was going to rewrite it, update it, and submit it as my next book.

It's easy again to say, in retrospect, that I had a feeling about this one, but I'll swear I did. The writing flowed, no hesitation, no mental blocks, just a glorious certainty as the words came spilling out on to the paper, and oh, how I enjoyed writing it! I then wrote down a dozen or so titles, and one sprang out – *Black Niall*. I typed it out – yes, I had learned by this time, dear readers – and sent it off. While I was waiting, I wrote two more: *Beloved Enemy* and *Master of Saramanca*.

On 23 October 1972 a letter arrived for me. It looked official. It looked like a Christmas charity appeal that had been sent out early, and I nearly put it to one side to be opened after husband and children had gone out respectively to work and school. But I didn't. I opened it and read those unforgettable, magic words: 'Dear Mrs Wibberley, we would like to publish *Black Niall* ...'

And now, read on ...

ONE

Excuses, Excuses … A Baker's Dozen

THE thought processes that go into making a writer are mysterious and wonderful. Equally so are the thought processes that go into the making of a *non*-writer who *is* going to write a book one day, and would love to be an author, but …

Some people have a writer's block before they even begin. They dream of being writers, they talk non-stop about the subject, they attend writers' conferences and carry important-looking notebooks and folders around and impress naïve newcomers no end. But they never actually *write*.

If you are one of these, this chapter is dedicated to you. And when you've finished reading it you won't have a leg to stand on so you'll have to start writing, won't you?

I'm starting with the all-time classic excuse than has been heard by successful writers on their travels more than any other. It is, of course, this:

1. I have no time … I'm too busy … too many other things
to do.

With an excuse like that, you're sunk without trace before you begin, so why are you reading this book? I mean, you don't really have *time*, do you? Of course you have time! You just have to make it, that's all. And you have to make it by being crafty and devious, if necessary. But what you really mean, I suspect, is: 'I can't be bothered to get started. It seems like too much effort.' That's nearer the truth, isn't it? Admit it, and the first hurdle is over. The second hurdle will be overcome by writing down everything you do in one typical day in your life, with times, from the moment you get up in the morning to the hour you curl up in bed. See? You weren't really working at other more important things, were you? What about the two hours you spent having coffee and biscuits with Mrs Thingy next door? Well, you had to call because she'd watered your plants and fed the cat while you were on holiday, and you were taking her a bunch of flowers, and she's a nice old dear, a bit lonely so you'd feel guilty if you spent less than two hours — hold it! Spend one hour with her and then introduce her to that other elderly neighbour you also feel obliged to visit. They may get on so splendidly that they won't notice you. Then there are the little shopping trips you make every week, approximately four hours in all. Go once a week, halve the time, buy a freezer if necessary, add that to the hour's visit you saved, forget about cleaning the windows this time, another hour saved. They'll need doing next week anyway so put them out of your mind until then, keep the TV firmly in the 'off' position, never mind *Pebble Mill* and *Take the High Road*. That is five hours you have to play with, so off you go. Everyone has some leisure time, even those who have a full-time job. If you haven't there is something wrong with your lifestyle. Use that time constructively. Put this book down at once and go and begin your romantic novel while the ideas are hot. You can pick this up later. The ideas might not be there later on, but this will. Off you go.

2. I couldn't bear it if my manuscript was rejected.

So you're frightened of failure, you poor thing. *So is everyone else.* There are some successful writers about who have never had anything they ever wrote rejected, but not many, believe me. For the vast majority of all kinds of writers all over the world, success only came after rejection. They didn't give up, I didn't give up, and neither should you.

  Let's imagine you have written your first romantic novel. You think it's absolutely perfect, as you should. After all, you've written it, you have presumably enjoyed writing it, and you gave it your best. Your friends have read it — even your enemies grudgingly concede it's not bad (high praise!). So now, tremulously, and with fast-beating heart, you have walked into the post office, handed over your precious bundle of neatly typed pages and gone home to begin your second book.

You wait. In between waiting you dart out to watch for the postman by the front window at the time he is due every morning. (Let us presume that this is, of course, after a couple of months. Don't expect overnight miracles with publishers. When you have been into a few offices and seen the stacks of manuscripts waiting attention you'll know what I mean.) You may even decide that, if you see him approach clutching what looks suspiciously like that envelope you had enclosed for the return of your manuscript, and it looks *heavy*, you won't even open the door – postpone the evil hour, as it were. But, anyway, there you are, one day, and here is the postman, and – oh, no, can it be – is that the package? You decide not to be a coward and go to the door. And it is. With a letter. A nice letter, pleasant in tone, slightly apologetic perhaps. But still saying, when translated, 'No, we don't want this. Thanks, but no thanks.'

Now. And this is the important bit. It is what you do next that counts. Remember the old saying (or I might just have made it up. It sounds very good anyway): 'It's not what problems you get in life that matter, it is how you cope with them.' You have several choices here. You can:

(a) Fling the manuscript and letter into the dustbin and vow never to write anything again, or
(b) Go and have a jolly good cry, or
(c) Get your list of romantic-novel publishers, parcel the manuscript up again and send it to the next one with a brief letter, or
(d) Sit down, have a cup of coffee and phone a sympathetic friend, or
(e) Put it to one side and get on with the other book, *determined* that this one *will* get accepted.

I do not recommend (a). I'll tell you why in a minute. I do recommend (b) as good therapy, followed by a brief session of (d); top is (e), to be followed in a day or so by (c). Got the order right?: (b) – (d) – (e) – (c).

Back to (a). If you put your typescript in the dustbin you'll never get it published because, so far, while science has advanced considerably in the last few years, no one has yet invented a robot that will sift through the rubbish on a dust cart and find unpublished manuscripts with potential and send them off for you.

Never throw anything away that you have written. Find an attic or a cellar, or a large suitcase if you have neither of the first two. When you pick up a rejected manuscript after a period of, say, a year, you will certainly see it through new eyes. The time-lapse will make it seem like something written by someone else and you will be able to read it with a fair amount of objectivity. And you may immediately see what is wrong with it and then be able to do something about it.

Even if, after this objective reading, you realise that it is pretty hopeless, do not despair. There may be some gem of a minor character, or theme, or background that would work well in another book. Out of my seven rejects, I've cannibalised several – and you can't be accused of plagiarism of your own work!

So do not be frightened of failure. Instead, regard a rejection as a stepping-stone on your way to success. I speak from experience. I regard my seven failures as a form of apprenticeship. And when success came, I was ready for it. I knew I could write – I'd done so much of it, after all!

3. You have to be lucky to succeed. I'm not lucky like you.

Someone once said to Henry Ford, 'Isn't your son lucky?' 'Yes,' replied H.F., 'and the harder he works, the luckier he gets.'

Sit in your little mental ivory tower and whine about your failure and how luck passes you by, and it will, it will. You have to go out and meet it more than half-way. Another definition of luck is 'Opportunity meeting readiness.' I could moan that I've never won on the football pools, but as I never fill in a coupon, it's hardly surprising.

I was at a writers' conference last year, and led a discussion group on – guess what – the romantic novel. The hall was crowded with would-be writers, all asking extremely searching questions, and at the end of the discussion I opened my big mouth and said, 'Right, all you would-be romantic novelists, the conference finishes Friday but I have to leave tomorrow [Thursday] afternoon. If anyone here wants to write, between now and tomorrow, the first 2,000 words of a romantic novel, I promise I will read it and give it an honest criticism.'

The discussion finished amid a buzz of excitement and I could see pens being unsheathed. Ah, well, I thought, thinking's one thing, doing is another, and I went off to afternoon tea quietly confident that I would have two, or at most three manuscripts pushed into my hands. Silly me!

What happened next was startling, to say the least. Long into the night, and the following morning, women were to be seen scribbling frantically on benches, sitting against trees (it was hot and sunny), crouched on the garden steps, huddled in corners. Lights burned late in attic bedrooms. I was handed not two, not three, but *twenty* manuscripts. It took me a couple of weeks to read them, but I did it.

Two lessons emerged before I left the conference. One girl enclosed an apologetic note with her (excellent) manuscript. 'I am writing this at 6 a.m., sitting cross-legged on my bed, so please excuse writing.' – that was neat too. About an hour before I departed for home a large important lady, who is going to write the best-ever romantic novel one day (or so she has been telling everyone for years) came up to me and said, 'Ah, give me your address, will you, Mary. I haven't had time to do anything here, but I'll have a go when I get home.'

'The challenge was for *now*,' I answered.

'Well, yes,' she conceded, with a little smile, 'but *I've* been too busy.' She had been too busy sunbathing by the pool – I had seen her.

I gave her an equally sweet smile. 'Too late,' I said. 'Sorry.'

Her voice echoed after me as I walked away. 'But what if I need some help?'

Now. Which of these two women do *you* think is more likely to succeed? Answers on a postcard please.

4. It's a closed shop, I've heard. They don't want new writers nowadays.

I've heard this old chestnut not once but loads of times, and I still don't believe it. The sheer illogicality of it takes my breath away. Let's imagine for a moment that it is the absolute truth, that publishers stopped wanting new writers in, say, 1900. Therefore the only books sold by bookshops would be written pre-1900, and the novels would nearly all be reprints of Jane Austen, Dickens, the Brontës, and other Victorian authors.

In fact, as everyone who ever wanted a book would undoubtedly possess all they needed of these, there would be no *need* for bookshops.

By the same token, all the libraries might as well close down, because everyone would have read everything. But hold on. Bookshops flourish, libraries flourish, second-hand bookstalls flourish – and with what are they stocked? With hardbacks and paperbacks written and published in the last eighty years, nay, the last twenty, ten, even two! And some of the writers weren't even born as long ago as fifty years. How can this be, you ask? I'll tell you how. These books have been written by men and women who didn't know that no one wanted them, so they took a chance and wrote a book and sent it off to a publisher and had it accepted. And they were *new* writers. And then they went on to write more, and got those accepted, until they ceased to be classed as new writers and became established. And they all lived happily ever after, dear reader, because they didn't use daft excuses that have more holes in them than a faulty colander. So don't you, either. Of course publishers want new writers. What they want is *good* new writers. And it's up to you to be a good writer. And if you read everything in this book, you will probably be one. End of lesson.

5. I'm too old to start. It takes years of work to succeed.

If you are over 104 then it *might* be possible that you would be better advised to knit a sweater instead – or perhaps, on reflection, a pair of mittens – but anyone under that age has no excuse at all. In 1972 a woman called Alice Pollock, who was 103, had her first book, about her Victorian childhood, published. More recently a woman of ninety-three had her first book published. At the other end of the scale, Daisy Ashford wrote *The Young Visiters* at the age of eight. I think we are all somewhere between those two extremes, aren't we? That being the case, age is no deterrent.

The second half of this excuse has as much validity as the first. It will take years for you to achieve instant fame and fortune if you don't get cracking, and twitter on instead. On the other hand if you begin *now*, today, this evening, and write 'Chapter One' on a new sheet of paper and let it go on from there, you could have everything neatly wrapped up in three months, accepted in five, on the bookstands some time next year, and you'll be one year older than you are now. All right, it might not be so immediate. It took me seven years. I didn't know that at the beginning, of course. It wouldn't have made a scrap of difference if I had. It might have prevented that glorious uncertainty though, but that was half the fun. So, if you are ninety-three, get started *this minute*. If you are any younger, be of good cheer. Have a cup of tea first, and *then* begin.

6. My friends think my writing is wonderful. Why doesn't it sell?

And that is lovely, of course, but your friends aren't really being very helpful, are they? The first thing is that they lack objectivity. They like you, and wanting (subconsciously, perhaps) to please you, they read what you have written whilst wearing rose-tinted spectacles. You would be better showing your work to someone who doesn't like you! There is a saying among gardeners: 'Always get your roses pruned by your worst enemy.' Seriously though, this is where a good writers' circle can be of help. I mean the kind which has published writers among its members, those who are prepared to say fairly where you've gone wrong. Listen. You might not agree with all they say, but at least listen. That is the first step in being able to take criticism.

When I submitted my first manuscript to the RNA after joining, the detailed criticism Helen MacGregor sent me — let's be totally honest — hurt just a little. She had seen all the weaknesses in my writing and told me what they were. After that first reading of her remarks, I sat down, read them again, took a long cool look at my manuscript and realised just how right she was. Then I wrote and thanked her and said I would rewrite on the lines she suggested, and did. She had taught me a valuable lesson.

7. I will start writing/dieting/exercising/etcetera – tomorrow (or the day after).

You are a procrastinator, that's what you are, and to save you looking up the meaning, I will tell you. 'To put off till some future time; to defer.' I know what it is to be a procrastinator – and how do I know that? Because I'm going to start exercises tomorrow, that's how I know; I made that decision after a visit to a health farm last year – and the tomorrow still hasn't arrived. But we're not talking about my procrastinatory problems, we are talking about yours. And you won't start writing tomorrow, and we all know it.

Tomorrow is so close, only twenty-four hours distant, but alas, also a world away. It never arrives. Only today is here. (Excuse me, this has jogged – if you'll pardon the pun – my conscience, all this talk about putting off. I've just done ten touch-toes, honest, and oh, I feel better for it.)

So if you are going to begin writing tomorrow, you won't. Make that today, now, this minute. Do it. Come back to this book when you have written your first 500 words and, like me, you'll feel much better. There is a story by Patricia Highsmith called 'The Man Who Wrote Books In His Head': I know tons of people who write books in their head. They are wonderful books too, all they lack is the essential translation onto paper. One thing about it is of course that you can't get that kind rejected, but then excuse number 2 will solve that for you.

8. I've no typewriter, no study, no workroom.

This is quite a good excuse for not writing. But, alas, not one which will hold water. You do not actually *need* any of those things. There are three essentials for writing and they are these: pen, paper, and your fertile imagination. And it doesn't take a genius to work out that these three requisites can be accommodated on a park bench, a kitchen stool, a bedroom (feet up on the bed, several pillows at back – very comfortable), dinner table, settee, or even − in extremis, with hungry children crying, dogs barking, and general chaos − loo seat (lid down!) in locked bathroom. I speak from experience. I have written on them all. I now have my own study with a magnificent desk and books all around me. And where will you often find me writing? In the garden if it's sunny, or at the breakfast bar in the kitchen (nearer the kettle, you see).

A writer is the most fortunate creature in the world. The artist needs his studio with a good north light, and easels, and tons of paints and brushes and palettes and smocks and probably a living model, or at least a bowl of fruit. The sculptor has to have that huge block of marble delivered and hauled up three flights of stairs, or loads of messy clay, and kilns for firing. The chef needs his kitchen, with pots and pans and *fines herbes* and truffles, and ovens at the precise temperature for the soufflé/roast/gâteau, or disaster will strike.

While you? All you need can be carried in your handbag or briefcase. The only trouble is, of course, that as there is not much impedimenta to lend a look of importance to your work, concerned elderly relatives have frequently been known to ask even highly successful writers if they wouldn't prefer a 'proper' job. Perhaps writing is an improper job. That's a new way of looking at it, anyway.

9. I've had no education. Friends would laugh at my presumption.

If you are managing to read this by yourself, you have had some education. If what you mean is: 'I've never been to university' join the club. There are writers with university degrees and there are writers without, and the ratio is probably 1 : 10. But what all writers have in common is a love of books − an insatiable appetite for the written word, which is probably of more use than any degree from Oxbridge.

If you can't spell, get a good dictionary. If you are such a rotten speller that you wouldn't even know where to look to find out what you can't spell, get the bad spellers' dictionary (there is one). If not, buy a tape-recorder and learn how to dictate your romantic novel.

If you have difficulty handwriting, join an adult education class, but remember Christy Brown while you are feeling sorry for yourself. He wrote *Down All the Days* with his *toes* because he was almost totally paralysed, and that fact didn't stop *him, because he wanted to write*.

Friends would laugh at your presumption? What friends are those? Strange friends indeed. Real friends are supportive, the kind of people you can let your hair down with, and relax with, and share problems with so that they immediately seem less important. They won't laugh, I promise you. If you have the kind that would laugh, ease them swiftly out of your life because they are not friends and never will be.

I collect sayings and mottoes from outside churches, from old magazines, from just about everywhere, and there is one that I read on a noticeboard once outside a church in the centre of Manchester. Just seven words. 'Empathy is your pain in my heart.' True friends have empathy. It is a lovely word. Remember it.

10. I live in Manchester, not Monte Carlo – and anyway, there have never been writers in my family so how can I hope to suceed?

So you don't live in an exotic location? And you think that all successful writers do? The law of averages decrees that there are probably a few romantic novelists and other successful writers who live in the South of France, and Spain, and the Caribbean. I have met hundreds of writers in the past fourteen years, all of whom live and work in Great Britain. You'd be surprised, but you have probably got one living just a mile or so away from you. Many of the ones I have met have never been abroad, or only once or twice in their lives. It has never held them back when it comes to the colourful backgrounds though. It's certainly never stopped me. I have never been to a remote tropical island, or to Finland, or the Gulf of Mexico, or the Caribbean, or Brazil. But I have set books in all those places. I have been to Monte Carlo, to Rome, to Paris, to Moscow, and to Amsterdam, and so far I have not set books in any of those places. Perhaps there is a lesson there somewhere. Maybe we can write more vividly about a location we have never visited. All to do with that glorious world of our imagination, perhaps.

And there have never been writers in your family, you say? So what? What on earth has that to do with *your* writing, pray? I come from a long line of teachers and headmistresses, so I should be educating a class of unruly ten-year-olds if I felt obliged to follow the family tradition, instead of doing what I enjoy most. Strike out. Be brave. If *you* want to write, go ahead and do it.

11. They don't want the kind of books I want to write.

First – who are 'they'? The whole world? All publishers? Just one or two? The public at large? The amorphous 'they' covers a multitude of sins – and excuses – in every walk of life. (' "They" should really do something about litter in the streets.' Why don't you? A friend of mine, fed up about it in her road, organised a sponsored litter collection. She felt good afterwards as well she might.) However, back to the 'they' who don't want *you*. Oh, I see, it's one publisher, is it? And he rejected your precious firstborn. Tell me, did you send your romantic novel/sci-fi/history of the world/whatever, to the correct publisher? Had you checked up first in your *Writers' and Artists' Yearbook*, and in the library, on all the books published by (let's say) Jack Brown Ltd.? If you had, and yes, he published exactly the kind of book you had written, and still rejected it, did you then find another two, three, four, a dozen publishers who also publish books similar to yours? Frederick Forsyth had *The Day of the Jackal* turned down by quite a few publishers before it found a home, and the rest, as they say, is legend. He didn't just put it away after that first heartbreaking 'no' – he simply sent it out again, and again, and again. So, get cracking.

12. I don't know any other writers.

Nor did I when I started writing. There aren't so many about when you're only three or four. I still didn't know any at the age of thirty when I wrote that first novel with the intention of getting it published. But there were at least two things I could have done. One was to have joined a writers' circle, which only several years later I did. The other would have been to start my own writers' circle. How, you cry? Well, I've seen it done, so I'll tell you. Write a letter to your local paper. Say that an aspiring writer (you!) wants to meet other aspiring writers. Then sit back and wait for a shoal of letters. That is how quite a few writers' circles have begun over the years. Some, alas, fade away after a few meetings, but others flourish like the green bay tree. In 1968 an advertisement appeared in the *Aberdeen Evening Express* asking for anyone interested in writing to attend a first meeting with a view to forming a writers' group. Half a dozen people turned up at that initial meeting, and from it there came into being the Aberdeen Writers' Workshop – which is still going strong seventeen years later, and with many highly successful writers among its members. Your library will tell you if there are any existing writers' groups in your neighbourhood. And if not, get out your pen and letter paper ...

13. I don't know how to start or sustain a novel.

I've left this until the last because I'm a coward. It is so awesome in its immensity, this problem, is it not? It make me tired just to think about it. There is however one little magic word: STAMINA. Without it you may be able to begin your romantic novel, but you certainly won't be able to sustain it. Writing of any kind is *very hard work*. It is both physically and mentally tiring. To look after the physical side, go on a high-energy diet now: bags of fruit and fresh vegetables, and bran every morning, and fish. Cut out the stodge, all those lovely fish and chips and squishy chocolate cakes and steak pies. (You'll lose weight too, isn't that lovely?) If you are already underweight, get on to Horlicks every night; you'll sleep like a log and it used to put pounds on me – but I woke up alert and alive and raring to go. Right, that's the physical stamina side taken care of, now what about the sheer mental grind of actually composing something like 55,000 words?

The longest journey (even that climb up Everest) has to start at your front door. You take one step down the path, and then the second ... And the longest stretch of writing you've ever attempted has to begin with the words 'Chapter One'. Set

yourself a target every day. Decide what you can comfortably do
– say, 2,000 words. That's not very daunting, is it? In
twenty-eight days, writing 2,000 words each day, you will have
written 56,000 words: a book.

Ah yes, you say, that's all very well, that sounds easy, but how
do I keep the action going, the characters living and breathing,
things happening? Oh, *that's* your problem is it? Well, this is where
a book plan would help. Before you even begin, write a
synopsis. You will, of course, have already written detailed
biographies of your main characters, and briefer ones of your
minor characters, and made a plan of the house where most of the
action takes place, or if not a house, the tropical island, or the
city. Details will be clear in your mind not only of your
protagonists but of the background where they live.

A synopsis does not have to be adhered to rigidly, in fact when
the characters come alive and take over, as they will, it will be
altered considerably, but if you have a framework, *you will feel
more confident before you start*, and that is half the battle, believe me.
Then mull things over for a few days. Incidents will pop into
your mind at the oddest moments, while washing up, walking
the dog, or gardening. I get a lot of ideas when I'm lying back,
steaming gently, in a hot bath. Write them down *immediately*.
(The paper gets soggy in the bathroom, but never mind.) Soon
you will have a nice stack of jottings, ideas, snatches of dialogue,
descriptive matter – the flesh to go round the skeleton. You will
have things to aim towards, and to get to them, you have to
write in their direction, and lo, the time will pass and you will
suddenly discover you are further on than you thought. *Don't
look back*. Like the climber half-way up the mountain, don't look
down, look on, upwards, ahead, keep going. Keep that thread of
continuity running strongly on. The time for correction is at the
end of the 56,000 words; then you will have something concrete
to chip away at. You will have a book.

TWO

Pardon Me, You're Treading On My Fantasy

BEFORE we get down to the real nitty-gritty of writing the romantic novel we have to get one thing straightened out, otherwise it will hang around in the background like the spectre at the feast.

Sooner or later all would-be romantic novelists are going to run into the inevitable cracks about romantic novels being escapist rubbish, the fantasies into which women retreat when the real world gets too much for them. So we'll examine a few myths about romantic novels and in the process learn a little more about just how widespread these knocking trends are in our society, and, I hope, knock them in turn!

First of all, romantic fiction is a long way from being a new phenomenon in literature. It hasn't always taken the form of a novel, as these are comparatively new, but romantic *story-telling* has existed since the dawn of time in one shape or another. Samson certainly paid a high price for his grand infatuation with Delilah; and what about Helen of Troy? 'The face that launched a thousand ships.' The Greeks certainly went to some lengths to win her back!

Nobody accused Homer of pandering to the romantic tastes of his readers when he produced his epic poem, did they? A recent article in a learned literary magazine identified the three major themes in medieval ballads as being war, romance, and the supernatural.

Shakespeare frequently wove strongly romantic themes into his plays. Paramount is, of course, *Romeo and Juliet*, but there are others, not least *Twelfth Night, Antony and Cleopatra* and *The Taming of the Shrew*.

In the nineteenth century when the novel as a true literary form began to appear, came *Pride and Prejudice, Wuthering Heights, Under the Greenwood Tree, Jane Eyre*. It is easy to say that these are all great books which just happened to have a romantic element running through them – but it is this very aspect which is remembered by their readers.

The simple truth is that love and romance represent one of the strongest motivating forces in our society.

Women are a long way from being the sole escapists in their reading. How many men read war stories, or westerns, or spy tales, without identifying with the macho hero? Every assault on a Nazi-held stronghold or shoot-out in a dusty main street is quite likely to have male readers reaching for a grenade or checking the hammer of the Colt .44 slung low on their right hip! Men, cunning beasts that they are, conceal these trends by creating a smokescreen as war gamers or gun collectors. Imagine the attack that would be launched if we women played romance games. Now there's a thought ...

When Ian Fleming created James Bond back in the dim and distant fifties he was not only indulging his own fantasies for sport, good living and the shadowy world of espionage – with a dash of sex for good measure – he was unleashing on the world one of the most powerful fantasy figures in literature. In Bond he created a man who blended attraction and cruelty, a good guy who missed being a villain by only a hair's breadth. Millions of men identified with him, as they had done in the past with Richard Hannay, the Saint, Bulldog Drummond and an army of similar figures.

No one attacks men for their escapism, do they? At least we women can claim that our fantasies are relatively harmless!

More escapism? Try television – *Dallas, Dynasty, Hotel*, and *Falcon Crest* – for the visual kind. A wedding in *Coronation Street* or *Crossroads* evokes a genuine spontaneous response from viewers who must know, in their saner moments, that what they are watching is no more than a product of the scriptwriter's fertile imagination, yet the presents and cards flood in from all over the place. Several people wrote in to see if they could buy

Rita Fairclough's house when it was for sale! Twenty-four hours a day – if we want to – we can tune in on the radio to a flow of songs of young love, lost love, new love, old love, sad love, shared love, and, any day now, gay love. The newspapers and magazines do their bit with their showbiz pages, gossip columns and profiles of the beautiful people to spin a web of glamour round those stars who are often created by the very media in which they exist.

And one of the biggest sellers of fantasy is the world of advertising which tempts us with offers of this delight or that luxury at prices we cannot afford to refuse. Whether a holiday in the South of France, a dream kitchen, shiny new car or the latest chocolate bar, these products are served up with all the visual and verbal skill which the adman can muster. Nobody has ever dropped from a helicopter and skied down a mountain to bring me a box of chocolates – yet – but I live in hope. And if I were ever to be stranded at the side of a motorway (unlikely, alas, as I don't drive) I would hope to be rescued by that extremely dishy young man who spends the rest of his time munching Yorkies.

When you consider all those things, it becomes very clear that romantic novels are only a small drop in the ocean of fantasy in which we are all swimming. That should make you feel much better when some very superior person (usually male) comes up to you at any gathering and smiles condescendingly at you and says, 'Oh, you write romances, do you? Tell me, my dear –' they always call you 'my dear' for some reason, which is where I always draw myself up to my full height of six foot (in heels) and smile back at them because they are invariably smaller than me – 'Tell me, pray, how can you write books like that?' The tone in which they utter the word 'books' implies that only good manners has prevented them from using the word 'rubbish' instead. Don't be drawn. Smile, answer something on the lines of: 'Oh, I enjoy writing romances –' and move smartly away and find someone else more interesting to talk to because men like that are guaranteed crashing bores. I read a lovely true story in a woman's magazine a few years ago. Small woman, standing briefly on her own at a large gathering, was approached by a man with drink in hand who said, as a conversational opener, 'Tell me, my dear, what do you find to do with yourself all day?'

Little woman put finger to mouth, and simpered: 'Silly me's a judge!' I wish I'd been there.

I gave a talk at a literary society last year and during question time a woman asked, 'Don't you ever want to write a *real* book?' Amid much laughter I answered that I thought I already did. But I knew what she meant. She meant a *literary* book. By implication she also meant that anything which is escapist, pleasurable and easy to read is not literature. Shortly afterwards I went with a journalist friend to a session of Writers on Tour, which is sponsored by the Arts Council. There we heard three women writers give selected readings from their works and afterwards answer audience questions.

A fleeting — but scathing — reference to Mills & Boon and romance in general was made by one of them during this question session. I kept silent, oh foolish me, but afterwards went and read the blurbs on the covers of the books these authors had brought for sale. One was about an eighty-seven-year-old woman who decides to commit suicide and locks herself in a cupboard to do so. I wasn't sure why. Another concerned a gorilla that is bred from a human ovum and goes to public school. So *that's* literature. I had so often wondered. One day (when I have time) I am going to write a book about a one-legged Armenian transvestite who is forced to flee (well, hop I suppose) to a Tibetan monastery after being seduced by his lesbian dentist. I'm quite confident I'll get an Arts Council grant to write it. So, yes, lady from the literary society at which I spoke, I would like to write a *real* book. And that will be it. Or I might just build a pile of bricks.

It seems to me that readability is a dirty word in some circles. Obscurity is everything. I don't enjoy books which give me a headache as I wrestle with the ramifications of beautiful words cloaking an almost complete lack of plot. Give me a P.G. Wodehouse to curl up with any time for preference. I'm not decrying great literature, works which have stood the test of time, I'm talking about the pseudo-intellectuals who would have us believe that only their work is worth consideration and all else is as dust.

So don't be apologetic when you become successful and get your first romantic novel in print. What you are writing is escapist fiction and there is absolutely *nothing wrong* with that. Fairy tales have been with us since the beginning of time. Everyone needs fantasy in their lives. It is highly unlikely that we are ever going to meet a debonair, self-assured male of six-foot-four with dark hair, grey eyes and a hefty bank balance, *and* a sensuous smile, but dammit, we can dream, can't we? The trouble is, real men grow older, go bald, develop a paunch. The James Bonds of yesteryear are the lawnmower-pushing husbands of today. But not in a book. Grant James, six-foot-four, dark, etcetera, will always be thirty-five, always have that slightly cynical smile playing about his manly lips, causing maiden's hearts to flutter. Long may he live!

Arnold Bennett summed it all up beautifully when he said: 'Nearly all bookish people are snobs, and especially the more enlightened among them. They are apt to assume that if a writer has immense circulation, if he is enjoyed by plain persons, and if he can fill several theatres at once, he cannot possibly be worth reading and merits only indifference and disdain.'

You can't argue with success. Romantic novels *are* successful. They sell in their millions, and give pleasure to millions. Is there anything wrong with that? The answer is no. And now that's out of the way, let's get down to business.

THREE

The First Four Minutes

FIRST impressions count, and the first impression your reader has of your hero is the one that will stay with her throughout the book, so you might as well make it a real cracker while you're at it. You could introduce your hero thus: 'Boris Leander walked into the room. He was tall with dark hair and green eyes.' Well, now we know that he is tall and dark-haired, but there is no picture in our minds, just a vague blur. Let's face it, Boris Leander (or whatever the hero's name is) is *the* main character. It is the hero that the reader falls for, it is the hero who brings the book to life for her. And it is the hero that we, the writers, fall in love with, or should, *whilst we are writing about him*, because if we don't love him, how on earth can we expect our heroine to do so?

I've written forty-four books and I loved every hero whilst I was 'in' the book, living it, breathing and sleeping it. For me he was real. When the heroine was furious with him, so was I. When she cried I had to get out the Kleenex, when she had a headache – ouch! A writer's life is not easy. We should get danger money with the royalties. So, to get back to him, the man. He has to make an entrance, and an impact on the reader's senses. This is someone special. Let's make sure our reader is as aware of that as soon, or even sooner, than the heroine.

The heading for this chapter, 'The First Four Minutes', was the title of a book I read several years ago, written by a psychologist who made the point – very effectively too – that in all encounters with new people in our lives, lasting impressions are formed within the first four minutes of meeting. It struck me as being true then and still does today.

So let's see how to make Boris Leander more memorable. He was the hero of one of my books, *The Dark Warrior*. Polly Summers, the heroine, is a journalist. He is an elusive tycoon who hates journalists and has always flatly refused to be interviewed, but Polly's editor, using a little gentle blackmail, has 'persuaded' her to go to a reception planned in Boris Leander's honour at the village hotel – using her resemblance to Boris Leander's late wife as a ploy to gain his attention and, perhaps, that precious interview. She is stuck in a corner of the large room, with several local dignitaries, all fussing over the imminent arrival of their important guest, and trying desperately to look like an ordinary citizen and not a journalist – he is reputed to be able to spot them a mile off – when there is a flurry of activity from the hall outside …

The mayor, a small pompous builder, came in first, wearing his chain of office and clearing his throat importantly. 'Ladies and gentlemen,' he announced, 'Mr Leander is on his way in. Please – no fuss.' He looked as though he was going to make a fuss. He looked as though he might burst with pride.

Polly's neighbours began talking quickly, the woman patting her hair, saying: 'Do I look all right, George?' and her husband, straightening his tie, turning to Polly.

'This is a big moment for Wallington,' he said.

'Indeed yes,' she murmured. She had no tie to straighten, and she wasn't going to pat her hair. She just wanted to go home.

Then he walked in. She had seen only a photograph of him that had been taken ten years previously, in his heyday as a racing driver, and that had been slightly blurred, but it was unmistakably him. It was as though everyone faded away, and she saw only him. He was tall, taller than anyone else there, and he was dark, and tanned, and devastatingly attractive. All man, immaculately dressed in grey suit, white shirt, dark tie. He stood there, looking round him, not smiling, and the mayor rushed forward, practically tripping over his feet to greet him, to shake hands – and Boris Leander looked across at Polly, and for a full five seconds his eyes were upon her. She felt as if she had just received a huge electric shock. Those eyes – She took a deep breath, and croaked, in answer to Mrs Potter, who had hissed: 'Isn't he handsome, my dear?'

'Yes, he is.' Handsome wasn't exactly the right word, but Polly was too transfixed to argue. Handsome implied smooth good looks, a big smile. His face was rugged and tough, the face of an adventurer – or a pirate; green eyes, sea-green, shadowed, a strong straight nose, wide mouth, hard chin. And he hadn't yet smiled.

The reason he had stared at her so hard for those few seconds is because – no, I'm not going to tell you. You'll have to buy the book.

In a very recent book, *Linked from the Past*, where I fell instantly in love with my Russian hero and wrote the entire manuscript in trembling anticipation – honest! – I had the hero make an entrance into the heroine's life in a totally different manner. Victoria Mitchell has gone to her uncle's vast and remote mansion in Scotland in winter, expecting to find her uncle waiting for her. He isn't, and she wanders into the darkened house, calling his name, goes into the large drawing room and is just looking, rather puzzled, at some books and papers written in Russian, on a table near the fire when she hears a slight sound:

She whirled round. 'Uncle –' the words she had been about to say died on her lips. A man stood outlined in the doorway, the light behind him silhouetting him sharply, and for a moment she had the illusion that she was seeing an old portrait step into life from the past, for there was something other-worldly about him. Then, as he walked forward, the illusion was shattered and she caught her breath in a strange, sick sense of recognition – equally quickly banished as she realised that she had never seen *this* man before in her life.

He spoke. He had a deep voice, as deep as brown velvet,

deceptively soft, and a strong foreign, instantly recognisable accent.

'Who are you?' he asked. Victoria took a deep breath, still shocked and surprised by seeing someone so different from her uncle.

'Victoria Mitchell,' she answered, equilibrium returning. 'And who are *you*?'

'My name is Gregor Shenkov,' the man answered. No possible doubt about the accent this time and as he walked forward, no possible doubt about the face, the high Slavic cheekbones, deep intense eyes under thick black brows, wide mouth that held no smile of welcome or anything else. And he was a very big man. He was tall and powerful-looking, broad-shouldered and narrow-hipped, wearing faded blue corduroy jeans and darker blue fisherman's jersey. She wondered, seeing him thus attired how she could possibly have taken him for a medieval man. Yet there was something timeless about his appearance, some haunting quality, an unusual blend that made her pulses race. He looked – dangerous, some adventurer from another world, as indeed from his name and accent he seemed to be.

And that was it, and during that description, I laid at least three 'clues' *that I was not aware of*, but which, as I continued to write, gradually fell into their place – and only then did I realise why I had done that. It is a strange feeling when that happens, a sort of shiver-down-the-spine feeling, and I thought, good grief, *now* I know why I said that. I had planned for Gregor to be the son of an old and valued friend of Victoria's uncle, who has come to Scotland to trace his family history. What I did not know, until much later in the book when my pen began to write the words on the paper, was that their two families were linked over a hundred years previously. One of his ancestors had married one of hers. And the reason for Gregor's shock on meeting Victoria was because he had, at his home in Paris (his father had defected there years previously), a miniature of his ancestress, who is the double of Victoria herself. And those two ancestor's names? Yes, you've guessed it. The Gregor Shenkov of all those years ago had married a Victoria Mitchell … There was only one possible title for it after that discovery: *Linked from the Past*. I did not know any of this when I started the book. I was just as surprised as they were when I discovered the link, I promise you!

Occasionally, sentences or phrases pop into my mind at the most unlikely times. I always write them down immediately which is often difficult because although I know every writer should carry a notebook at all times, I sometimes forget. The backs of my chequebooks are a constant source of surprise to my accountant, covered as they are with dozens of minutely worded notes. We were returning from the vet's once (my husband and me, not my accountant and me) after having taken one of our dogs for an injection, and I was struggling into the car in the rain, dog on lead, handbag in free hand, husband saying things like: 'Hurry up, I'm not supposed to be parked here –' when a man walked past, and the sentence 'He had the face of a buccaneer' sprang ready-formed into my mind. I managed to disentangle the dog, lead, and handbag, scrabbled for my chequebook and wrote it down before I could forget it. On that same chequebook cover is another phrase which did its obliging print-out across my mind when I was being driven to the shops by same previously-mentioned long-suffering husband (I never remember to carry a pen either, and have to borrow his and he gets annoyed when, for instance, he's trying to negotiate traffic lights at busy crossings). A teenaged youth was walking past with his girl-friend, both clad in jeans, and he walked with that cocky strut of so many young men of sixteen or seventeen – and came the four words, neatly printed across the inner eye: 'He had aggressive legs'. Well, he *did*. Whether I'll ever use that one is another matter. But it's there, if necessary.

So don't do as I do, do as I say. Carry a notebook with you wherever you are, even beside your bed. How many frozen winter's nights have I sat up, searching for pen and paper to write some immortal lines that were literally preventing me from going to sleep? Several hundred at the very least.

Someone took me to task about my heroes recently. She said they were too tall. Be less specific with your six-foot-three or -four hero, she said. They are too tall for your shorter readers – and she had a point there, I realise. I had never considered it before. Being tall myself, that is the height of my ideal man, and my heroines are always tall because I could not write from the viewpoint of a woman of, say, five-foot-two. We see the world – literally – from a different angle. So I asked a few of my romantic novelist friends of that lesser height how they felt about it. One said, 'Oh, I love 'em tall, mine have got to be over six feet.' Another admitted that she never specified a hero's height, and a third said that yes, she knew what I meant, but who would want a hero of five-foot-six? So, you take your pick. But it is worth bearing in mind. Having said that, we can only write what appeals to us anyway. Unless you write primarily for yourself your book will not come to life. *You write what you would like to read.* And what a glorious thought that is. When I was sixteen or so I read a book that had a profound effect on me: *I Capture the Castle* by Dodie Smith. I have tried to read it since, but that first wonderful magic was not there, although it is an excellent book. But the magic *was* there the first time that I read it, and the *memory* of that has remained and will remain with me for a long time, if not for ever. There are some books that you read at the right moment in your life, and their effect is far greater. This was one.

Let's get back to the hero, and the effect he has, not only on the heroine, but on the reader. Remember the old saying: 'Manners maketh man – and clothes maketh woman'. Clothes also maketh man, at least between the pages of a romantic novel. The impression created initially by you, of your hero, is very important, what follows is equally so. No good him making a stunning entrance if he tends to fade into the wallpaper later.

Last summer a startling thing happened to me in one of Manchester's more snooty stores. It started off a whole new train of thought about something I had known subconsciously but rarely considered on a conscious level. I was standing in the perfumery department trying all the perfumes as is my wont, with nary a thought of writing in my head. (I'd taken a day off from it, and, anyway, someone's got to buy food for my starving family. I just enjoy trying perfumes and make-up first.) Suddenly, and without any warning fanfares, there came striding towards me the most unlikely and dramatic figure I could have imagined. A man, almost seven feet tall, clad *completely* in black from head to toe. A long black cape swirled about this incredible creature as he strode through the shoppers, scattering them like so much confetti, neither looking to left or right. A magnificent, awesome sight. Customers gaped, assistants gaped, I gaped. The man was Darth Vador. 'What on earth's *he* doing in here?' I gasped when I could speak (which was fully five seconds later – writers learn to recover quickly).

'I haven't a clue,' the assistant to whom I'd spoken answered. 'But – my God! Isn't he just incredible!' I did what any right-minded scribe should do: I followed him out of the store. And there he was, standing outside on the pavement under the store's awning, signing autographs for a rapidly swelling crowd of children, while a man wearing a store's badge took photographs. I asked the photographer what was going on and he told me that there was a promotion in the toy department, that the man sweltering inside the outfit was the original actor from *Star Wars*, Dave Prowse, and that he had come out for a breath of air, though how he could see, let alone breathe, behind that mask, I had no idea.

I went off to do the rest of my shopping then, but several vivid impressions lingered. One the effect he had had on me. Another the effect he had had on everyone else. The third, and perhaps most important, was the effect of his attire. Let's forget the Darth Vador mask he wore. It was the long black cape, black top, trousers, boots and gauntlets that were the knockout. The effect was *electric*. The image of the man in black is a very powerful one. Think of Dirk Bogarde in the film *The Singer Not The Song*, Jack Palance in *Shane*, and dozens of others in thrillers and westerns. Sinister figures all. But in a hero, the sexual imagery is extremely potent. Whenever *Wuthering Heights* is mentioned, I visualise Heathcliff dressed in black. I'm sure a lot of people do. As I said, it's not something I had consciously thought about, but at some point in many of my books, I have had the hero dressed all in black, and the picture while I wrote was vivid in my mind. I'm not suggesting for a moment that your hero should spend all his time dressed thus, for the impact would be lost, but it is worth thinking about for certain key scenes.

Other clothes that create a macho virile image are denims, probably because of the association with lumberjacks, cowboys, etc. Again, jeans are the uniform wear of most teenagers of both sexes. Try a head count (or rather, a bottom count) sometime in a crowded street. But our heroes aren't teenagers, they are mature men. And I've seen some very dishy mature men in denim jeans and jackets. Corduroy, suede, leather – these materials for clothing have their part: use them. Avoid going in for long descriptions of your hero's clothes. Instead create the picture you want to put into your reader's mind in a couple of sentences.

This is where television comes in useful. Study what the heroes in films wear, make notes while the films are on and you will have a rich store of clothes to draw upon when you need them. A recent poll in America showed predictable results as far as we romantic novelists are concerned. The man most American women are looking for must be – wait for it – tall, dark-haired, blue-eyed, and built like an athlete. They didn't need a poll to discover that. The organisers could have saved themselves a lot of time and money by asking any successful romantic novelist. We've all been writing about them for years. The ideal man should also have expressive eyes and a dynamic smile, and that dark hair, so said most of the answers, should be curly rather than straight, and short rather than long. Hairy chests did very well, even though a small percentage said they preferred a 'smooth' man. (What? No hairy arms or legs?) Strength was important. Lean, slender types came nowhere at all, which is hardly surprising. If the heroine is about to be crushed by a pair of manly arms against a manly chest, those arms and that chest had better be muscular.

The women who answered the poll also said that they preferred their ideal man to be several years older, and well groomed. Tom Selleck, of *Magnum* fame, Christopher Reeve, alias Superman, and Richard Gere, were three of the names mentioned as fulfilling female fantasies. And if you ever see any photographs of that heart-throb of sixty years ago, Rudolph Valentino, you will realise that women's tastes haven't changed all that much in the years between.

The first four minutes are important. What follows must hold the reader equally intrigued so that when she reaches the end of your romantic novel, it will be with a satisfied feeling, and she will put the book down with the urge to go out and buy your next one. Your hero's behaviour and mannerisms therefore must be consistent with the image you have created in the first pages. I read a romantic novel recently where he was totally incongruous, one minute treating the heroine like dirt, the next trying to make love to her, almost immediately after that heaping scorn on her head – then pursuing her relentlessly. The heroine was confused, poor girl, and no wonder. She should have given him his marching orders pronto. He annoyed me so much that I skipped a great deal of the book. I imagine a lot of other readers did too. Only if your hero is real to you will he behave in character. And only if you, the writer, love him from the beginning – despite his apparent faults – will he come over as a warm, living human being. You can do it.

FOUR

Find The Lady

LIKE the Mounties, you've got your man. But what of the lady? The heroine, naturally. Later in this chapter we'll discuss minor characters and how valuable they can be in advancing your romantic novel, but for the moment it's ladies first.

The character of the heroine is at the same time easier and yet more difficult to put across to the reader than that of the hero. Confused? You won't be after you've read this. Easier because in a sense the heroine is *you*, so that it is a matter of projecting yourself, the woman you would like to be or indeed are; more difficult, because as the story is told from your, the heroine's viewpoint, it is extremely hard to describe her and establish what kind of person she is without occasionally resorting to a little trickery. It can be made clear very quickly that the hero is arrogant, bold and tough, and so on – all the things you want him to be, in fact – by his actions, by the way he speaks, not only to the heroine but to other characters in the book. It isn't quite so simple to establish the heroine's personality to the reader. It is essential to know the heroine's thoughts and feelings, her attitude to life, and a skilful blend of narrative and dialogue is needed. Once you, the writer, have established her firmly in your mind, she will (or should) behave consistently with that character. Before we see how this can be done, let's run through a few basic types of heroine that the readers like and can identify with.

Type One: The Cinderella

She can be an orphan, or one whose parents are divorced, and for various reasons, she sees neither of them very often. (Perhaps mother is a famous actress who doesn't want it known that she's old enough to have a daughter of twenty. Father is a ruthless businessman, remarried, who doesn't give a damn about her.) Cindy lives with an aunt who doesn't give a damn either, and makes her work hard for her keep. Cindy's life is pretty miserable, she is not encouraged to bring friends home, or indeed to have any. But she has a mind of her own and seeks ways to escape the drudgery of her everyday existence – perhaps by taking a job looking after a child, or as an au pair abroad, or simply by leaving home and finding employment in London.

Type Two: The Wealthy, Spoilt Playgirl

She has been everywhere and seen it all, is selfish and arrogant, and oh boy, is she heading for a fall. And the hero is the one who is going to teach her a well-deserved lesson, and of course, fall in love with her at the end of it. It is essential to bring in some quality in her that will elicit the reader's sympathies. You can't have apparently inexcusable behaviour on her part without a good reason – which you can tell the reader of course, thus giving her an insight into this heroine's character. This one is slightly more difficult than the Cinderella type, but has been used very effectively in many books.

Type Three: The Independent-Minded Free Spirit

This is one of my favourites. The girl who is positive and outgoing with a sparkling personality and a good sense of humour. She is naturally going to clash with the hero, particularly if he is as described in paragraph two of this chapter. Sparks will fly from the word go, because she isn't going to be bossed about by any man, is she?

Type Four: The Successful Model/Artist/Actress

She's attractive – and knows it – independent, and successful in her career. She is used to being admired by men and is therefore rather disconcerted when the hero doesn't fall over himself at first sight of her!

Type Five: The Equally Successful Businesswoman

She is also attractive – but may not be as aware of it as the previous heroine. She may also be slightly anti-men, because she has had such a struggle to reach the position in business that she holds now. I don't need to tell you that the hero will also be extremely successful in his chosen field, and that there will be, inevitably, a strong clash of personalities and interests before all is resolved at the end of the book.

Type Six: The Waif

Not to be confused with the Cinderella type, the waif is orphaned and has no one, not even an unpleasant aunt to bully her. In my book *Gold to Remember* Janna was living in dire circumstances in a small town in South America after being orphaned, and is rescued by Luke Tallon, and brought back to an England she has never seen. The only way he can get her back is to marry her, and they have every intention of having the marriage annulled once here. But things don't go according to plan ... I enjoyed that book very much. Waifs go down very well with the readers. But avoid any suggestion of self-pity on her part. She may be a waif, but she's a plucky one!

Type Seven: The Heroine-Who-Has-Lost-the-Love-of-her-Life

She could have been married, or engaged to him, but he has died, and she is desolate. No other man can match up to the one she has lost, and she tends to compare every man she meets with her late lamented. (Try not to have him killed in a car or plane crash. They have been overworked.)

Type Eight: The Disillusioned Heroine

She has had some very traumatic experience that has left her scarred. She is suspicious of all men, questions their motives, and will therefore be looking for similarities between the hero and the man who destroyed her trust – and no doubt finding them. He has a difficult job on his hands.

Type Nine: The Scatterbrain

The one who opens her mouth and puts her foot straight in it. The one who reverses her car into the hero's because she gets the gears confused, and who needs rescuing constantly by a growingly impatient man, who suddenly realises that life would be very dull indeed without this scatty young woman.

There are more. You may be listing several at this moment. The one that appeals to you most is the one to write about. But, remember, you must be careful not to overdo any of the characteristics of these heroines to the extent of making your reader irritated with them. For instance, the one who has lost the love of her life must not become a pain in the neck; the rich bitch must have redeeming qualities that are evident from the beginning; the scatterbrain mustn't be so scatty that the reader wants to shake her! Never make the reader feel uncomfortable.

The modern-day heroine needs a strong personality, a determined outlook on life, even a touch of the women's lib, if you like, but please, never make her wishy-washy. Ultra-feminine she may be, but not a female wally!

Right, you have decided what she looks like, but how do you tell your reader? An obvious way is to have her look in a mirror – which can be a cliché – and describe what she sees, or you can do it gradually, a phrase or two at a time over the first few pages so that a picture will be built up in the reader's mind so subtly that she will scarcely be aware of it. Readers do not want huge chunks of descriptive narrative. It's poor writing to have several paragraphs describing the minute details of characters, or setting, or anything else that is an integral part of the book. The reader's eye will wander, she will skip some, and she may miss something you would prefer her to know. So don't do it. You may do it, indeed you must, *before you begin writing the book*. You will write a very detailed biography of your heroine, and you will do it in the way that suits you best, and as detailed as you like, so that the picture of your heroine is firmly imprinted in your mind well before you write the magic words 'Chapter One'. Physical description is essential, of course. Without it you may well, in the heat of writing, find that the heroine's eyes have changed, inexplicably, from blue to green or even grey, and then you'll have to make corrections in manuscript or typescript, and you will have wasted time. After the physical description, write clothes, job, hobbies, mannerisms, even a family tree if necessary. Write her likes and dislikes in food, drink, books, animals, films – everything you can possibly think of, and you will be building up a picture of a person who becomes more real with every word. An example of what I mean will best illustrate this, but remember this is only a rough guide. You will be writing a biography of *your* heroine, for *your* book, and her life can only come from your fertile brain.

Eve Chalmers. Age: Twenty-three. Height: five-foot-seven. Hair: dark auburn, worn shoulder-length, thick hair with a natural wave of which she despairs because she would love to have it swept back in a dignified chignon sometimes, and it is too thick and curly and resists all her efforts. Eyes: deep grey, large, with dark lashes. Clearly defined eyebrows needing very little help from eyebrow pencil. Face: oval, well-defined cheekbones, snub tip-tilted nose – she envies the straight noses of the rest of her family, because she feels she always looks young. Warm generous mouth, white even teeth. Medium build, long slender legs, curves in all the right places. Clothes: makes some of her own. Good sense of style, likes wearing casual skirts and blouses, shirt-waister dresses, sandals in summer, fashion boots in winter. Favourite colours: soft blues and greens. Job: crafts. Supplies a friend who has a craft shop with pottery, lampshades, ornaments, small paintings and so on. Is very talented artistically. Education: Grammar school. Best subjects: Art, English, French; hopeless at Maths and History. Food: loves salads, fruit, chicken, chocolate mousse, marzipan; hates chips, steak, oysters, anything fried. Drinks very little. Hobbies: sketching, swimming, reading, skiing, cooking, gardening. Does not like housework. Faults: quick-tempered, occasionally over-sensitive. Family: widowed mother, elder brother and sister, both married with children. Personality: quick-witted, decisive, good sense of humour; patient (usually), a strong sense of justice; tends to leap in wherever she sees injustice being done. Has travelled widely, working as an au pair in two countries (France and Italy) for a while when she was eighteen, but has now come back to the small village in Derbyshire where she was born to help look after her mother who is recovering from a stroke. She works from home supplying the craft shop.

Such a detailed biography should give you a picture of a living human being, and, were you to embark on a novel with Eve as its heroine, would enable you to have her behaving in character right from the word go. You might prepare your heroine's biography in a totally different way. No matter – the only essential is that it helps you to know your character fully. So, the scene is set for Eve to meet the hero. A clue in the biography under personality, namely, a strong sense of justice, and under faults, quick-tempered, should see to it that in the conflict with the hero, who will undoubtedly be arriving in her village bent on changing it in some way, Eve will be in there, fighting!

I'll tell you how I got one of my heroines, a complete personality, full of a life of her own. It was in 1979, and I had recently finished a book, and was enjoying a break from writing, doing what any self-respecting author does between books – reading. I was also getting the itchy fingers that always presage a new book. One day I was watching television and an episode of a series called *Heartland* came on. The moment it began, my sixth sense told me to switch on the video, and I did. I knew immediately that the girl in the play was my heroine for my next book. Her name is Arwen Holm, and the programme began with her being helped by Donald Churchill (who also wrote the play, and excellent it was too). He played a gentle type of con man on the run from the police, who, as the first scene opens, is sitting in a field having a picnic lunch when he sees her car break down, and her anguished reaction to it. It turns out that she is on her way to her wedding rehearsal to a very wealthy man. I watched the entire play in total fascination, and then played it back and made comprehensive notes of every mannerism of the actress, a detailed description of her physical appearance, clothes, voice, personality. Two days later I began writing the book, called it

Fire and Steel and named my heroine Arwenna. If you're reading this book, Donald Churchill or Arwen Holm – thanks a million.

As far as your minor characters go, it does help if you have several eccentric relatives (particularly aunts, for some reason). They may play only a minor role, but, for adding life and colour, cannot be beaten. I'm fortunate in that not only did I have three gloriously and outrageously eccentric aunts, but quite a few nutty great-uncles as well. We don't choose our relatives, it is said, but if we did, I wouldn't have swopped those. They are no longer here, alas, but the memories linger on. One of my aunts, Bertha Walker, an older sister of my father, was one of the first women in Great Britain to hold a motorcycle licence. Somewhere in my boxes of family photographs is one of her in full fig – goggles, soft leather cap with chin straps (no crash helmets in those pre-1920 days), leather jacket and trousers. She was also a headmistress of an infants' school, wrote children's fairy stories, was a staunch vegetarian who served the most horrendous barley pudding I've ever tasted, and made pots and baked them in a huge old kiln, in her spare time. If I ever bought any clothes which were too jazzy in style or colour, I always passed them on to her. She didn't know the meaning of the word moderation in anything.

If you don't have relatives to draw on, do not despair, borrow them. Your heroine often needs a sympathetic ear in the midst of all her traumas, and an older woman relative is ideal. I 'borrowed' Margaret Rutherford for one of my books, *Beloved Enemy*. Remembering her in the role of Madam Arcati in the film *Blithe Spirit*, cycling through the village with cape flying, just filled the bill in that book. I'm sure she wouldn't have minded if she'd known! I've also used Finlay Currie (in *The Moon-Dancers*), and Burl Ives (once or twice in different books, as jovial uncle or grandfather!), and several other actors and actresses – or, at any rate, their interpretation of the roles they played – from the small or large screen. These characters, when you write about them must be as real to you as they are to the hero and heroine, or they're not going to be more than cardboard cutouts propped against the scenery.

Friends of writers often ask, 'Have you put me in one of your books?' The answer could easily be a cautious 'Well, yes and no', which they wouldn't understand; only another writer could. We can quite cheerfully cannibalise bits of our friends – and enemies – so that a complete character emerges made from several parts of several people. Sounds a bit like being a spare-parts surgeon, but if, say, you have taken the more unpleasant traits of several people you don't particularly like for one of your less endearing minor characters, no one is going to be able to sue you for libel, are they?

We are learning something all the time, or should be if we are not to grow stale. I'm a different person now from the one of twenty years ago when I wrote the first of my seven rejected books. I am different from the person who had *Black Niall* accepted in 1972. Being a writer is being involved in a constant process of change. Hopefully, as you go along, for the better. With experience in writing, as in anything else, comes improvement, a subtle difference in style, an expertise with words – a new depth to your characters, both major and minor. You will find it easier to say the things you want to say after four books, and easier still after ten.

FIVE

Adlestrop To Zanzibar

WHERE will you set your romantic novel? Paris, Rome, the West Indies, New York? The right background is very important in any book, perhaps more so in a romantic novel where a tropical island, for instance, being romantic in itself, can warm the reader before the book even begins.

Remember Adlestrop? Yes, I remember Adlestrop, the name, because one afternoon of heat, the express train drew up there unwontedly. It was late June. Hold it, that sounds very familiar, as well it might. Those are the first lines of a poem written by Edward Thomas, a poet killed in the First World War; ever since I learned that piece at school, aeons ago, it has stuck in my mind.

We aren't talking about poetry, though; what we are talking about is a background for a romantic novel, which could as well be set in a small village like Adlestrop as an exotic foreign location. The background is the stage on which your characters are going to act out their lives, so what appeals to you?

Consider two blurbs from the back covers of two contemporary romances side by side on the shelf of your local W.H. Smith:

Ethel met Alfred late one night in the canteen of the Wigan gasworks where both were employed. Love bloomed instantly among the gasometers and she thrilled to his touch – but who was the glamorous Hilda Brown? And why did Alfred lie to Ethel? Was their love destined to be destroyed before it had really begun?

Or:

> Tara went to Bermuda to work as secretary to the wealthy
> playwright Brent Vallon. There was an instant attraction
> between them, but along came the delectable Sonya who, it
> seemed, had a prior claim on Brent. Was it too late for
> Tara?

Which one would you be more tempted to buy? I hope you'll
say the second, or I'm wasting my time writing this chapter.
(Notice too the discrepancy in names? For further enlightenment
on that aspect see Chapter 11, 'A Rose By Any Other Name'.)

Obviously love does bloom in the canteen of a gasworks, just
as it does in offices, factories, supermarkets and everywhere else
that men and women meet. But in romantic novels the reader is
seeking escapism, and that can be more easily found in the places
we all dream about: a tropical island, the Highlands of Scotland,
the Lake District, Rome, Paris, Monte Carlo ... The list is long,
and if you write about a location that appeals romantically to
you, your heart is already there, and so, we hope, will the
reader's, if you are a skilful writer.

All of us have at some time stood and looked over a sunset
beach, misty landscape or a distant mountain, and longed to
capture the moment. Some people do, with cameras, or paints
and canvas. You will do it with words. Effective evocation of a
location is at the heart of most good novels. It is true that the final
success of a romantic novel lies with people and their
relationships, and how well you present them. But these liaisons
do not take place in a vacuum, they are played out against a
background which may well reflect their feelings. Could
Wuthering Heights have taken place in a suburban setting? Would
the gentle wit of Jane Austen have sparkled as brightly against
the wild grandeur of a Scottish island?

In romances, as in many other kinds of novel, an exotic
background appeals simply because it is so far away from the
normal environment in which most readers live. Yet there have,
of course, been equally successful romantic novels set in parts of
England, Scotland, Ireland and Wales. An elderly woman I
know, who is housebound, particularly enjoys romantic novels
set in remote, faraway places. She told me: 'I sit down to read,

and it's like going on a lovely holiday. I feel as though I'm taking a long journey without all the hassle of passports, and catching planes. It's a beautiful way to see the world.' I knew exactly what she meant when she said that, and I set my next book, just for her, on a Caribbean island.

There have been times when I've sat down at my desk, mind as blank as the virgin paper before me and thought – where on earth do I set the next one? A world atlas (borrowed from my children) is dragged out and put on the desk. Eyes closed, finger pointed, jab. Oh, no. The middle of Africa. Try again, Mary. China ...? Well ... just one more go. Oh! That's interesting. Brazil. What do I know about Brazil? Not a lot. This actually happened several years ago. Brazil, I thought. Well, I can't sit here all day jabbing at an atlas. So Brazil it is. My two children were at primary school then, coming up to ten and eight. And one of my son's classmates was a Brazilian boy. They played together, and I'd already featured the boy, called André, as a minor character in my first published novel, *Black Niall*. Although I'd only briefly met his mother at the school gates she was very pleasant, though shy. I telephoned her and asked if I could talk to her about her native country. I told her why, of course, and she invited me round to their flat. So off I went that evening clutching a notebook and two pens. (Yes, I do remember sometimes.) I staggered home several hours later loaded not only with very copious notes but also magazines, photographs and lists of names. Enough for a very comprehensive background, the kind which could not be found in any books on the country, but which painted, for me, an authentic picture of Brazil. In fact from that first visit, and from subsequent ones, I gained enough background material for four books.

There's a great deal more to choosing a setting for your romantic novel than opening the atlas and sticking in a pin. The golden rule, according to so many writing textbooks, is that you should draw upon places with which you are familiar as raw material for your backgrounds. But, as the previous paragraph demonstrates, you don't have to stick to the rules.

Now, before you say no one could set a romantic novel where you live, there's a good chance someone already has. Taking a broader view of novels, you will find that almost every corner of Britain has been used as a setting for a book, from Neil M. Gunn's Caithness, to Daphne du Maurier's Cornwall. Robert Louis Stevenson used Edinburgh settings; John Braine, Yorkshire; Walter Greenwood, Salford; Arnold Bennett, the Potteries; Thomas Hardy, the West Country (his 'Wessex'); and nearly everyone has used London.

So it doesn't matter where you live – countryside, village, town or city, the potential is there for you to set your novel. The appeal will lie in what you make of that setting, whether it's a Scottish castle, a Thames houseboat, a West End hotel, or a converted water-mill. How, therefore, do you create a successful setting? A place itself is only so many buildings, or hills, or trees. Why do thousands of people walk the same streets, or explore the same woods, and yet only one in a thousand will bring the places to life with their writing? The simple answer lies in the capacity of those chosen few (including you, the writer) to see things in a very special way.

In an interesting experiment some years ago, half a dozen top photographers, men who command hundreds of pounds for a single session, were given modestly priced cameras and sent out to photograph whatever they wished. The results were startling. In spite of the technical limitations of their equipment, each man produced work of striking quality. The object of the exercise was to demonstrate that the ability of these photographers lay not in their cameras but in their talent for capturing the essence of what they saw through their viewfinders.

In your writing you must seek the same quality, and try to convey not only the streets, buildings, and landscapes in plain detail but also breathe life into such scenes so that the reader is, for the duration of your romantic novel, transported to a French château, or a London mansion, or a sailing schooner off the West Indies. The readers will savour the tang of the sea air, and breathe the scent of wild flowers, or feel the snow crunching underfoot.

In my books I have used English settings more than any other, with Scotland running close second, followed by France, Brazil, and islands of the Indian Ocean in almost equal numbers. The Gulf of Mexico, a Greek Island, and Austria have featured once as settings.

On one occasion several years ago, I took a manuscript to my publishers, and having absolutely no idea about the setting of the next, said to Alan Boon, 'I haven't a clue where to set my next book. Any suggestions?' to which he replied, 'Why not try Finland?'

That was a bit of a facer. I knew next to nothing about the place, apart from the fact that Helsinki was the capital, and Laplanders lived in the north of the country. Hardly an auspicious beginning! So I came home, went to the library, determined to borrow all the books on Finland that they possessed. The search did not take long. There were just two! Finland, it seemed, was not one of those places that inspired a great many travel writers. I brought the two books home, read them and gained a few facts. *But* ... in one of them was a paragraph headed: 'Autiotupa, or Wilderness Huts.' And from that one paragraph I gleaned not only the basis for my plot but the title. I called the book *The Wilderness Hut*, and that's exactly where I set it, in the heart of Finland.

The paragraph went roughly like this (it's ten years ago since I read it, so my memory, not being eidetic, could be slightly faulty). 'Autiotupa or wilderness huts are scattered throughout Finland. Located specifically for use by hunters and travellers, they are simple wooden huts with a large fireplace, a table, two benches and a raised sleeping platform in one corner. They are free, and the only requirement is that travellers replace any logs they use for the fire, and leave the hut in a clean condition.'

That was it, but it sparked off the vital idea that gave me the entire plot; following that I borrowed a *National Geographical Magazine* full of beautiful colour photographs of the scenery and the Laplanders. I also read a thriller set in Finland and visited the Finnish Consul in Manchester who was extremely helpful and gave me more material. I was also fortunate to find that a friend of a friend had a Finnish wife, who sent me a list of Finnish Christian and surnames, and a number of phrases.

The only task that then remained was to write the book! The odd thing is that now, whenever I see anything set in Finland on television, I feel as though I have been there, and have to remind myself that I haven't. I felt as though I was actually there when I wrote *The Wilderness Hut*.

Let's consider how you can go about finding settings that will appeal to you for the books you are going to write. The most obvious source of material is your own experience, both here and abroad. Whenever you go on holiday, make notes, collect leaflets, keep a travel diary and, of course, take photographs. The setting may not appeal immediately as a romantic background, but at some future date, when coloured by nostalgia and warm memories, you could see the place through new eyes. Foreign visitors that you meet can give you a valuable word picture of their country (remember my Brazilian friends). What they can provide are the rich details of everyday life that you would rarely gain from any book. Cultivate such encounters, and remember that these people will delight in telling you of their lives. We all love to talk about ourselves! The travels of our friends can also be a joy. The holiday photographs and slide shows you once dreaded should now be welcomed with cries of delight. Think what that will do for your popularity. You may well be the only one not to fall asleep on such an evening. Rather you might cry: 'Run them through again, Cedric, I missed the first fifty!'

You will, of course, be a member of your local library, and know the full resources they offer – travel guides, first-person accounts by seasoned travellers, encyclopaedias and gazetteers. The junior section will yield further treasures in the form of both novels and non-fiction books that are not only clearly written but usually beautifully illustrated. Two examples of children's reference books that can be found in bookshops or libraries are the *Collins Children's Encylopedia of the Arts of the World*, and *The Sampson Low Great World Encylopaedia*. Both crammed with illustrated details of people, places, cultures, flora and fauna.

The much-maligned television opens windows on the world with stunning impact. Make notes – better still, buy a video. Many first-time visitors to New York, for example, experience a sense of *déjà-vu*, arising from the wealth of TV programmes which have featured that famous city. The same can be said of London, Paris or Rome. I feel that I know San Francisco for the same reason (my husband loves *The Streets of San Francisco*). From all of these you should have the backgrounds for your first hundred romantic novels. After that you may have problems.

Very often, places have about them a sense of romance that

may be ready made for your purpose. Many writers regard the Scottish Highlands as just such a setting – mist-filled corries, sweeping mountains, and the solitary shape of a golden eagle soaring high against the sharp blue of a summer sky. When I was thirteen, staying with my uncle and aunt in Wester Ross, I observed the Northern Lights as a curtain of greens blending into silver. Totally unforgettable. But in the hands of a skilled writer the flat waterways of the Norfolk Broads can be made just as romantic. A few pages of Paul Gallico's *The Snow Goose* will illustrate this.

Some cities are photogenic and have about them a definitely romantic atmosphere – London, Edinburgh and York, to take three – but I recently heard a friend's account of her barge holiday through the heart of Birmingham, and she made me see that city from an unusual and quite romantic viewpoint. What does this prove? Basically, that our ideas of romantic locations are likely to be intensely personal. Your task as a romantic novelist is to convey your feelings for a place to the reader in such a way that she too will be enchanted with it.

Atmosphere is as important as background. Consider the following three settings and then think about the effect they will have on your characters' behaviour.

First, an island in the Indian Ocean, the sun blazing down from a cloudless sky onto golden sands. A beach cabin with palm-frond roof, surrounded by coconut palms swaying in a slight breeze, colourful wild birds darting overhead, the distant throb of music with a strong drum beat. And your hero and heroine walking in from the sea, she wearing a sarong, he in brief bathing trunks, skin glistening gold and drenched from the salt water, and there, in the shade of the palms, a table set with cool drinks, but to get to it they have to walk across the burning sand ...

Then, a Hebridean island in autumn. Mist swirls round a two-hundred-year-old cottage that has walls three feet thick. Inside, a log fire burns, sending sparks up the smoke-blackened chimney, and an oil lamp on the table hisses, lighting the room palely; the heroine, sitting on the hearth rug, clad in a warm Fair Isle sweater and tweed skirt, strokes the cat beside her, and looks up as the hero enters the front door, bringing in with him the icy coldness, his hair damp with mist. He closes the door, and looks at her ...

A villa in the South of France, overlooking the Mediterranean, a large white building surrounded by lush trees, purple bougainvillaea cascading down the wall overlooking the swimming pool. Early evening, fairy lights strung out among the trees, sleek cars, Rolls-Royces and Mercedes and Porsches, lining a long, winding drive. Inside, chandeliers blazing a thousand lights in a huge hall, catching the diamonds worn round the women's necks and upon their fingers. Outside, on a stone-flagged terrace, the heroine in a long black dress, standing looking out towards the sea, holding a champagne glass in her hand, unaware of the tall, dark-haired man watching her from the shadows ...

Remember too the five senses. The sound of church bells ringing in the distance on a frosty winter morning; the scent of flowers; the taste of fresh orange juice; the gentle caress of sea on skin; the sight of a towering mountain – all evocative of things with which your reader is familiar and can therefore feel immediately she reads the words.

Over a hundred years ago, Gustave Flaubert wrote the following unforgettable words: 'It is a delicious thing to write, to be no longer yourself but to move in an entire universe of your own creating. Today, for instance, as man and woman, both lover and mistress, I rode in a forest on an autumn afternoon under the yellow leaves, and I was also the horses, the leaves, the wind, the words my people uttered, even the red sun that made them almost close their love-drowned eyes.'

Live in *your* world while you are writing. Be a part of it, with your characters, love them, laugh and cry with them. When the book is finished it will be like saying goodbye to old friends. And something else: it will be like returning from a journey to another place, so real that you will be able to go back there any time you want to. Perhaps you will, in another book.

PS: Zanzibar. Island off East Africa joined with the former state of Tanganyika to form Tanzania: cloves, coconuts, copra. Capital, Zanzibar. That's all I know because, as yet, I have not wanted to set a romantic novel there. However, you might ...

SIX

Keeping The Plot Boiling

NOW it's confession time. This is a chapter about plotting, as you will have remarked from its title. I am going to come clean. I know nothing about plots. End of chapter. No, I'm sorry, I'm just joking.

I will put that in a different way in case you think you are wasting your time reading this part. When I begin writing a book I do not know what is going to happen. I have not worked out any chapter in advance, therefore each day that I sit down to write brings new surprises. This is not the case with many writers who like to have a framework before they begin, which is also a good idea, as long as they are prepared for the inevitable changes when the characters come to life and take over. This is a point which I make frequently in talks to writers' groups and at conferences, and it bears repeating. Too rigid a structure will inhibit your writing because you may feel bound to adhere to it. Don't try. Part of the discipline in writing comes from knowing when to let go and relax.

First, I'm going to tell you how a book came into being for me, from the first moments of conception. After that, we'll go through a general, very flexible framework for a possible way to structure your books.

The Moon-Dancers was my sixteenth book, and I wrote it in 1975. The idea for it had been triggered off by a programme on television about the evacuation of the island of St Kilda, and an incident that had happened to me some sixteen years before gave me the title. Two things, totally unconnected, that became a book. I found the TV documentary absolutely fascinating, and was making notes before I went to bed on the night I watched it. Supposing, I thought, I were to set a book on an island similar to St Kilda, have the heroine as a sociologist who goes out to see if the island, like St Kilda, should be completely evacuated ... and suppose there is a hero who lives on the island and who resists her every move strongly ... and suppose ... so it went on. When a book is about to take shape, when ideas are forming, the world is full of 'supposes'. It is a wonderful sensation, this playing about with fragments of ideas, places, incidents; a very satisfying feeling. Suppose the heroine (I hadn't yet got to the stage of names for anyone, this was still only an idea) feels it wiser to go there in some sort of disguise?

I went to bed and slept on it, and as usual the good old subconscious mind did its work overnight, and when I woke the following morning more ideas came rushing at me from all sides as I sat down at the table. Soon I had several pages of extremely quickly jotted notes. There would be a bird sanctuary on the island. The hero would run a hotel at which ornithologists gathered ... the heroine would pretend to be a bird watcher, to enable her to look round the island more freely ... there would be a legend – well, I like legends, especially if I've made them up. And this is where the incident of all those years before came in. I'd gone away to the seaside for a weekend with Derek shortly after we were married. We were walking back to the hotel along the promenade and I stopped to look at the sea. The moon was shining on the water, and as I watched, a strange thing happened. I can see it again now as I write this. I know it was an optical illusion, a trick of the moonlight, I know all this and I knew it then, but it does not alter what I *saw*. It was as though people were dancing in the waves, round and round, couples dancing an endless polka in a vast silent ballroom. It was eerie and haunting, and completely unforgettable. I wanted to tell the world, to let them see what I could see. Wisely perhaps, I refrained. But in a strange way it hurt me, *because I couldn't do anything about it*. I couldn't share the beauty because no one else would have understood. It was only when I began writing books that I knew I could do something about those images – and many more – that were stored in my brain. But from that particular incident came the title *The Moon-Dancers*, and, with the telling of a legend in the book, the ghosts were exorcised.

Gradually as I began to write that morning, names came to me, and the descriptions of hero and heroine, he to be called Grant Mackinnon, she Lory Stevenson. I sketched a rough plan of the island, of the hero's house, and of the village. But as yet I had no minor characters. That didn't matter. I was prepared to wait to meet them when Lory arrived at the island – and I would also find out then what else was going to happen. And so the book began with just four things: the setting, the two main characters, and a legend. At what point would I start? The best point to begin any book is when a change occurs in the life of the heroine. Where better to begin, then, than with her departure, suitably 'disguised' in respectably dull clothes, hair scraped back into an unflattering bun, from London to fly to Creagdubh? As Lory was being seen off by her father, it was simple to begin with an explanation, during their pre-flight conversation, of her reasons for going. I knew that the first surprise awaiting her would be the hero. But I didn't know what other surprises lay in store for her. I had to wait for her to arrive to find them out. The plot unfolded, almost like watching a play on television, *as I wrote*. I 'saw' what was happening, and I wrote down what I saw.

Lory was expecting to stay at the hotel run by an elderly, woman-hating Scot called Mackinnon, with whom her father had done battle years previously. But old Mackinnon has died, and it is his great-nephew who meets the plane, and the group of ornithologists, including Lory. He found out precisely who she really was at the beginning of Chapter Two, and from then onwards it was a battle of wits. He decided to teach her a lesson, to make her see that his island, and his people, needed no outsiders telling them what to do. And slowly Lory began to see the place through his eyes, and to sense the fierce loyalty of those people she met.

From that point onwards I was an interested observer on the island as additional minor characters and incidents completed the plot.

There's no new thing under the sun, so it is said, and that certainly applies to plots for a romantic novel. It has also been said that there are only seven basic plots in the world, and as these are based on the seven deadly sins, they don't apply to romantic novels. (You can hardly have a slothful hero or heroine, can you? Although I dare say if one of the minor characters was extremely lazy, and the heroine was employed as companion/secretary to her/him, you'd have the germ of an idea. I hand it to you free.)

So if there's nothing new under the sun, and all the possible variations and permutations will already have been used by someone else, not once but hundreds of times, how can you think up something original? The answer is, you can't, so you might as well stop worrying about it. What you can do is make your approach refreshingly different, your characters full of a sparkling life of their own, and then you have a new book. Obviously some themes have been used more than others. The girl who goes to be a governess to the hero's son or daughter is a popular one. This can be abroad, the hero either British or some other nationality; or in Britain itself, and there are often complications in the person of the other woman with whom the hero appears to be in love. Another theme has the heroine left some property in a remote place where there is some man already living there who resents the heroine going to claim her inheritance, either because he wants to buy the place himself or because he considers she doesn't deserve it. Whatever the reason, there's trouble, you can bet.

The heroine is either blackmailed into pretending to be the hero's fiancée or into marrying him, and the conflict starts there. The heroine may be orphaned and put into the guardianship of the hero, who clearly resents her intrusion into his life and makes it plain. (This one is less popular these days.)

The heroine may go to work for the hero as secretary, and he has the reputation of being a womaniser, or she is forced to work for him to save her father or brother from the folly of their gambling or bad investments and past stupidities in some field. The heroine may have lost her memory and be told that she has married the hero, and she does not know whether this is true or not. The heroine may decide to revenge herself on the hero who has in some way wronged her family. An eccentric will may mean that the heroine is forced to marry the hero but purely as a marriage of convenience – or at least that is what they both intend it to be. The list goes on and on and the variations are almost endless. They are all tried and tested and have not been found wanting, so don't worry about the task of finding a plot that has never been used before. They all have.

Decide which idea appeals to you and which you want to write, and set down the basic requirements. Remember that the idea which has particular appeal to you is likely to be one which you will do well ... in exactly the same way as the setting which holds special appeal for you is likely to catch your reader because of your sympathetic handling of the setting.

The most basic romantic formula must be the Cinderella story because it contains so many of the ingredients of the ideal romance: beautiful, downtrodden orphan cruelly treated by her stepmother and horrendously ugly sisters, living a life of drudgery. She meets the prince at a ball (with the kindly intervention of the Fairy Godmother) and they fall in love. But something goes wrong and she forgets the time. Suddenly she realises her beautiful clothes are about to change back into rags and she flees from the palace, leaving behind only her slipper. (I often used to wonder why that never changed back into rubbish. Never mind.) The prince then spends a lot of time searching for this beautiful girl with whom he has fallen madly in love. The search ends happily after one or two hiccups on the way. Exit stepmother and ugly stepsisters and much gnashing of teeth and serve 'em right. Exit Cinderella and Prince towards a rosy future. Ahh!

Update that plot and what could we have? A beautiful but penniless orphan lives with her horrendous aunt and two ill-mannered brats of daughters. (Her uncle, the aunt's husband, is nice enough, but unable to cope with the combined pressure of his domineering spouse and children.) Then, out of the blue, arrives a tall dark attractive man to rescue her (Prince Charming and the Fairy Godmother rolled into one. But, if you want, you can have an updated Fairy Godmother). And he will take her off to his villa in the South of France. And I've just realised that I've used that plot in *Man of Power* where the hero, Morgan Haldane, a very wealthy hotel owner from the Riviera, comes to England to see the repayment of a debt owed by his father to her late father (who had been comrades-in-arms). As she is an extremely spirited girl he sees her potential in helping him beat off the attentions of a woman who is causing him a great deal of embarrassment, and provides her with a house at the same time.

When I started that particular book I had no idea I was using the basic Cinderella theme as a springboard, but it worked out magically all the same. This same plot can be worked on over and over again for various levels of society and in various places. Another old favourite, and not just in Mills & Boon novels, is the Romeo and Juliet theme which was not original when Shakespeare used it, and has been used a goodly number of times since then. (One thing about Shakespeare, he knew a good plot when he saw one. And he saw and used a good number that belonged to other people.)

If you think of all the romantic stories you have read, there must be lots that have struck you as belting plots for use at some time. Don't hesitate to jot down the outline of a good plot when you see it for future use. Many writers, particularly in the short-story field, build up their own encyclopaedia of plots.

But where else can you find plots for your novel? Well, one of the best sources lies in your daily newspaper where you'll find situations every day which would be ridiculed as too fantastic to be used by any editor. I wonder when you last read a story and thought how odd it was and how anything like that could happen.

We spoke earlier on about some of the situations which might provide the heroine with the problem she must overcome. What about the business of odd wills? You think these only happen in fiction. Don't believe it for one minute. I have read stories of wills and legacies which were so hedged in by qualifications that you wonder if the money was ever passed on. Talk to any lawyer and he can probably give you instances, without mentioning names of course, of cases he has handled and the odd aspects of the wills in question.

Or how about eccentric tycoons and millionaires? If you think that the heroes in some romantic novels are incredible and none would ever behave like that, just try reading the biographies of some of the great millionaires. Remember Howard Hughes and his strange behaviour? Believe me, you could make your hero/tycoon as odd as you want and he would still pale into insignificance beside some real-life counterparts.

Or again, if you think that the idea of the heroine being tricked into marriage is a bit far-fetched in this day and age you should have a read of some of the divorce proceedings in the press and catch a glimpse of the reasons for the divorce and the private lives of the parties concerned. There's the raw material for a dozen novels in any one week's papers.

At this point it's important for you to remember what we mean by plot. The theme of romantic novels is clearly laid down because they are romantic novels: in other words they should feature a romance, but not a romance which is scheduled for a happy conclusion right from the word go. If so, there is no story but simply the repetition of what happens in people's lives every day of the week.

What provides your plot as vehicle of this theme is the obstacles which prevent the fulfilment of this romance and which must be overcome before the romance can be brought to its conclusion. These obstacles, the stuff of life of plots, arise out of character reactions and attitudes, external forces, rivalry or any combination you wish. Remember that the biggest obstacle of the plot lies in the characters of the two protagonists (what a fine word that is!). The hero is usually an extremely macho individual, the heroine liberated and independent and knows exactly what she wants. Therefore, in their clash of personalities you will have conflict – an essential part of any novel, romantic or otherwise. Remember if it were not for conflict there would be no book, so it won't hurt to repeat it. If a hero and heroine meet and fall in love on page three, and continue to be blissfully happy from that moment on, you will have a book, of a kind, but it won't be a romantic novel as we understand the term. Shakespeare summed it up very neatly in *A Midsummer Night's Dream*: 'For aught that I could ever read, could ever hear by tale or history, the course of true love never did run smooth.' Another quotation from the same play is also apt: 'Lord, what fools these mortals be!'

So as all human beings are fools, and as the course of true love is rocky, the stage is set, isn't it? Also, invariably the hero and heroine don't realise they love each other – or if they do, fight it like mad – another cause of conflict in itself. Let's consider a few causes of conflict between man and woman that may trigger off ideas for you.

Family feuds: Their families have been at loggerheads for years.

Cultural differences: Spanish or Italian hero with fixed ideas of women's role in society.

Attitudes to money: He's a capitalist, she regards money as far less important.

Conflicting jobs: He's a property developer, she's a conservationist.

False assumptions: He thinks she is a gold digger (mistakenly, of course).

Lifestyle clash: Spoilt rich bitch meets tough, rough diamond.

Again, you could have a situation where the hero is put in the position of having a hold over the heroine. Such a hold may be financial in origin; her family has a debt to discharge in order to avoid court proceedings and ultimate disgrace; or the hero is her employer and consequently regards her as a subordinate; or the hero has inherited her family's land and she has to try to win it back; or the hero has been employed by her family to 'look after her' in some capacity – as a bodyguard, instructor, or guide. Whatever the situation may be, the potential for conflict is there because of the relationship which is imposed on the two people.

Take your pick from these, or make your own list. Either way, if you have your characters bang to rights, the dialogue and narrative will sparkle with their own electricity. I was once in a bookshop, doing one of my unofficial on-the-spot surveys and got into conversation with a woman who was choosing several Mills & Boons. I pretended I was buying some as well. I once made the mistake (when I was very new, and green, and thrilled to see my books on the shelves of Boots) of telling a fellow browser among the romantic novels that I was a writer for Mills & Boon, and had in fact written that very book she had just decided to buy, and she looked at me in stony disbelief, said, 'Oh, yes, really?' and moved away very smartly to the checkout to pay, and fled from the shop. I learned my lesson. I've never done it since. So, browsing, I got chatting to this pleasant middle-aged woman and asked her what she liked in romantic novels, and she confessed with a smile and a little reminiscent sigh: 'Ooh, I *love* it when they're *fighting* all the way through.' With her in mind, I've tried to see that mine did, more or less, ever since. It's *fun*. There is something very exhilarating in writing the kind of scene where your hero and heroine are – metaphorically speaking – squaring up for battle with each other. It gets the adrenalin flowing wonderfully – and what's more, it makes the love scenes, when they arrive, that much more potent and heady.

I appreciate that my haphazard method, the I-wonder-what's-going-to-happen-today one, might not appeal to, or work for some of you. So perhaps the more structured way will. You could try plotting your novel chapter by chapter in advance. Write a synopsis, but make it flexible enough to allow the characters to develop of their own free will. Remember, as your writing progresses the plot may take twists which you didn't plan originally; if your synopsis is too inflexible such developments may be frustrated. If that sounds too serious, let me put it another way. Your characters will take on a life of their own and do, or say, things that may surprise you. This is all part of the glorious uncertainty of writing – believe me, *they* know what they are doing, and that will be the moment to revise your framework and let these living, breathing people get on with it. It's happened to me, and other writers, so often. Even as I've written a sentence, I've thought, I didn't know *that* was going to happen! – and the book has taken a total new turn. It is a wonderful feeling. You'll know what I mean when it happens to you.

SEVEN

First And Last

Grab your reader in the first page, in the first paragraph; if possible, in the first sentence. Why? you cry. I'll tell you why. It's because if you go into a bookshop, or a library, and pick up a book, the first thing you do is read the first few sentences on the first page. If you don't like them, then more often than not you'll put the book back on the shelf, and that's that. It may be the best you would ever have read, but you're not going to find out, because it didn't grab you immediately. It did not make you want to read on. If you don't believe me, go and stand in any bookshop on a busy Saturday afternoon and watch the browsers browsing. And do a bit of market research yourself while you're there. Pick us as many books as you like and see how the opening words grab *you*.

Before I go into the ways to begin your romantic novel, let's study the beginning lines from some of the books I have in my library. Not necessarily romantic novels, but the ones I read and enjoy in between writing. (Every few months I have to have a clear-out or the books would take over the house and there'd be no room to sit down, let alone do anything else.)

First, of course, that wonderful book that so influenced me at the age of sixteen when I discovered its magic, *I Capture the Castle* by Dodie Smith.

I write this sitting in the kitchen sink. That is, my feet are in it; the rest of me is on the draining board, which I have padded with our dog's blanket and the tea-cosy. I can't say that I am really comfortable, and there is a depressing smell of carbolic soap, but this is the only part of the kitchen where there is any daylight left. And I have found that sitting in a place where you have never sat before can be inspiring – I wrote my very best poem while sitting on the hen-house.

I bought A.N. Wilson's *Unguarded Hours* on the strength of this opening sentence: 'Had the Dean's daughter worn a bra that afternoon, Norman Shotover might never have found out about the Church of England; still less about how to fly.' That is priceless.

And Monica Dickens' *My Turn to Make the Tea*, about her hilarious and chaotic life as a journalist: 'The telephone rang. I picked it up, glad of something to do, for there was not much stirring in our office that afternoon, except the spoon in Joe's teacup.'

This is an absolutely superb eight-word opening sentence from Mary Stewart's *The Gabriel Hounds*, a romantic suspense novel set in Lebanon: 'I met him in the street called Straight.'

Another romantic suspense by Catherine Gaskin, *Edge of Glass*, begins thus: 'Sometimes when I see a scrap of paper blown before the wind I am reminded of the way he seemed to come into the shop that morning – almost soundlessly, with only the stirring of the draught from the door causing me to look around.'

I read recently a haunting and highly readable book by a comparatively new writer; I was hooked by the first sentence, and the book, like the others I have just given as examples, lived up to that first promise. I simply could not put it down. *The Eyes of Darkness* is written by Leigh Nichols, whom I must admit I had never heard of, but she's now on my list of authors-to-look-for-in-bookshops. This is how it begins: 'Shortly after midnight, just four minutes into Tuesday morning, on the way home from a late rehearsal for her new show, Tina Evans thought she saw her son, Danny, in a stranger's car. But of course, Danny had been dead for more than a year.' I was hooked from that sentence on. I lose quite a lot of sleep that way, if I make the fatal mistake of picking up a good book at about eleven at night!

What do all these opening paragraphs have in common? Whether serious or humorous, they share one quality. That of making the reader desirous of knowing what is going to happen next. A very wise Mills & Boon writer, the late Clare Bretton-Smith, whose pen name was Hilary Wilde, once told me at a writer's conference: 'Get your hero in on the first page, the first paragraph; the first *line*, if you can.'

As a direct result of that advice the opening lines of my first accepted book, *Black Niall*, went: 'Nobody knew that Niall MacBain was coming home to Shielbaig until the stormy summer day he arrived.' A sentence of which I felt quietly proud, I can tell you. And even more so when that wonderful letter arrived from Mills & Boon to say they were accepting it, and I danced round the house at 8.15 in the morning shrieking wild eldritch shrieks, causing children and animals to flee in disarray – *and* my husband was shaving in the bathroom at the time. Have I told you that before? Tsk, tsk, it was not a pretty sight, the blood-spattered creature wearing dabs of toilet paper at strategic spots on his cheeks and chin who came down minutes later.

'They're publishing my book!' I yelled, and he replied calmly, 'I always knew they would.' Which was the biggest lie in the history of the world, because it was he who, during the days of my seven rejects, had urged me to take up knitting, 'because at least you'll have something to show for it.' When I reminded him of those words a second later, he answered with a kindly smile, 'Ah yes, I told you that because I knew it would be a challenge to you – and you see? *It worked*!' Thus neatly taking the entire credit for my success and demolishing any further argument. That man is a genius, as well as being a male chauvinist *par excellence*. It had got to the stage when I would be writing a book mid-afternoon, say, whilst looking after my dear infants, while all about me rejected manuscripts hurtled through letter boxes, and I would hear Derek's key in the door, and hastily stuff the said manuscript down behind a cushion and spray the room with furniture polish, and he'd come in, and take a deep appreciative sniff and think I'd been doing housework (silly man) and as the children were too young to give me away, I lived to write another day.

Still, this isn't getting us anywhere with opening sentences, is it? One of my best-selling books, *Lord of the Island*, had an opening sentence mentioning the hero even sooner than in *Black Niall*.

This time he begins the book: 'He was big, lean, and dangerous –
Sally Herrick knew that instinctively the first time she set eyes on
him. But she didn't know who he was – not then. She didn't find
out for several days, by which time it was too late.'

So it will pay you to study as many opening lines from as
many romantic novels as you can, decide which ones grab you,
which ones don't – and analyse why. If the paragraphs at the
beginning of any book make you catch your breath, they are
good. If you have to read several pages before you begin to have
a clue as to what is going on or who the main characters are, then
the writer has failed to grab your interest, and that five pages
may be all you will read of her book. Hook your reader at the
beginning, make her think, as she opens the first page to skim
down it, 'Hmm, this looks promising,' and before you can say
'Contemporary romance!' she'll be sitting at home with her feet
up, ignoring the pile of ironing in her kitchen, lost in your
world, with your people, having a thoroughly enjoyable time.

A mistake made by many aspiring writers is to feel they have
to tell the reader everything about their heroine in the first few
pages, to set the scene, as it were, for the action that follows. I
beg you to refrain from this course of action. The heroine's life
story can emerge gradually, while the action is taking place, thus
involving the hero more directly. A friend of mine once
remarked, when we were discussing romantic novels, 'The book
is only really alive for me when the hero and heroine are
together.' It's true in a sense. Oh, I know that there are passages
where the hero is absent, but there is a buzz going whilst the two
main characters are locked in battle, or making love, or simply
talking – or there should be. You have two strong personalities,
you love 'em both, they're in a situation involving conflict – of
course there are sparks flying. So don't waste time at the
beginning. Get the hooks into your reader so that she becomes as
much aware of this fact as you do. The writing will flow faster
too.

Let's suppose a new writer begins her book thus:

CHAPTER ONE

Kate Morgan looked at her watch as she left her house. She

hoped that her car would start. It had been snowing on and off for days, and although the main roads weren't too bad, the tiny avenue where she lived was like a skating rink. She sighed. Her boss wasn't the easiest man to work for, and she had been unavoidably late the previous day due to her mother having one of her funny turns. It had all been so different when old Mr Somers had been managing director of Somers Industries, but three years ago he had retired and now –

'You won't be late home tonight, will you, my dear?' Her mother's voice came from the doorway of the house and Kate looked back and waved to her.

'I hope not,' she answered. 'Don't stand there, it's too cold. Remember what the doctor said – you must keep warm, with your chest –'

'I just wanted to be sure. I'll have your dinner ready at six. Mind the roads now –'

'I will. 'Bye.'

Kate drove through the snowy, busy streets, urging her little car on, worrying about her mother. Celia Morgan, widowed three years previously after a blissfully happy marriage, was a frail woman who rarely went out despite Kate's urging, seeming content to stay at home and embroider or watch television, which made any kind of social life difficult for Kate because her mother worried so. How she had changed in those three years, from a happy fulfilled woman to the timid creature she was now. Kate gritted her teeth as a large car swung out in front of her. 'Oh, damn,' she muttered. That was all she needed. And the lights had changed again. These lights were always bad. They seemed to get stuck in favour of the main road traffic. She tapped on the steering wheel, seething with frustrated impatience as a heavy lorry manoeuvred itself out from a side road, scraping past her with inches to spare. There was a meeting of the Drama Group tonight. Providing there was something interesting on television, her mother might not mind her going too much. The only trouble was, Kate was invariably made to feel guilty whenever she told her mother she was going out, even for only an hour or two. It was difficult to put into words *how* she did it, but –

And so on, for at least five pages of Kate's journey to work during which it may or may not become clear that Kate's mother is a pain in the neck, that Kate's boss is also a pain in the neck, for different reasons, and that she will very probably face his wrath when she arrives. Poor Kate! She is, of course, a spirited lass and will cope with these problems – but that will emerge gradually during her confrontations with her as yet unnamed boss, as should the fact that her mother is a raging hypochondriac also emerge gradually and painlessly as the story progresses. But by the time Kate at last reaches her office, the reader may have lost interest. So, a better place to begin? Try this.

CHAPTER ONE

'You're late – again,' Jake Somers said flatly.

Kate Morgan dropped her car keys on her desk, and looked at him. 'So I am,' she answered. 'And I've had a hell of a journey here, *and* I'm frozen. But I can assure you I'll be working in two minutes, if you'll just let me get my coat off.'

He looked at his watch, then at her. 'See that you are,' he answered. 'We've a busy day ahead of us.'

'Haven't we always?'

He had turned away and was about to go back into his office, but paused. 'Something wrong?' he enquired, in the kind of tone that always made her hackles rise.

'Now that you ask – yes,' she retorted. 'I'm five minutes late – *five minutes*. If you go down to the typing pool you'll see there are three girls there out of twenty. The roads are icy, the buses are running late, I set out twenty minutes earlier to get here on time and you're standing there with a stopwatch –'

'I don't have one,' he cut in calmly, a slight smile playing about his mouth. 'So how –'

'Oh, go to hell!' Kate yelled, and to her utmost horror, burst into tears. There was a sudden shocked silence, then:

'Go and wash your face, get yourself a cup of tea – and

be back in five minutes,' he said. His door closed. Kate was left staring at it in dismay. First the scene over breakfast with her mother, and now this! Slowly, shakily, she sat down and found a handkerchief ...

The action and conflict have begun on page one, and will hopefully continue right the way through the book, and you can tell the readers all about Kate's mother *later*. The important thing to establish at the beginning is the relationship between Kate and her employer, the formidable Jake Somers.

And now to endings. 'This is the way the world ends,' we are told by T.S. Eliot in 'The Hollow Men', 'not with a bang, but a whimper.' He was not talking about books. We are. And our books should not end with a whimper, should they? They should end gloriously, happily, satisfyingly. The reader should be left feeling good, because if she does the chances are she will promptly go and buy or borrow another of your books.

The happy ending in a romantic novel can be satisfying without being twee. Obviously, at the beginning of any romantic novel there is hostility between hero and heroine for various reasons, part of it lying in the fact that they are both strong characters with individual tastes, points of view and preferences, and unwilling to concede anything to the other. In the course of the novel some degree of compromise must be achieved, yet without forfeiting these character traits which make them individuals. In fact, the romantic novel ends like so many real-life marriages continue: with adapting to others. This sounds very serious, doesn't it? But the point I'm trying to make is this: romantic novels suffer a lot of criticism for being divorced from reality, but in many ways they embody reality. As I said, the endings don't need to be twee, but they do have to be happy – and part of the success of this lies in the tying up of loose ends.

A recent speaker at a conference I attended claimed that some television plays which leave the viewer with unanswered questions are better for that, because they are more like life, which is full of unresolved endings. Rubbish! A book, play, or film, for reader or viewer, should be *a complete experience*.

It's all very well to say life is unhappy, full of continuing conflicts, loose endings, dissatisfaction, and so forth. But the reader comes to a book expecting a degree of escapism from these aspects of life. You would feel cheated watching a western that ended with Clint Eastwood and Jack Palance walking towards each other with guns cocked, and you would not enjoy a detective story where the murderer is still unknown on the final page. Furious letters from frustrated audiences and readers to film companies and publishers would follow!

So study the endings with as much interest as you study the beginnings of the romantic novels you enjoy (and those you don't), and see how the writer deals with them. Did your book take place upon a tropical island where hero and heroine were shipwrecked for 189 pages? (If it did, will you write and tell me the title? I'd love to read it.) You don't really want them to be stranded for the rest of their lives, do you? Well you *might*, but the other readers, including me, would prefer to know that they were going to return to civilisation to get married, so where better to end than with the arrival of the rescue boat?

> He took her hand, and together they watched as the motor launch set out from the huge liner. 'This isn't the end,' he murmured. 'It's the beginning of a new life for us – together.' She looked up at him and smiled. Together. It was a lovely word.

THE END

Don't pinch that ending, will you? It's just given me a marvellous idea. I think I might use it, or something similar. You can go and make your own up, which is what you intend to do anyway, I know.

EIGHT

A Word In Your Ear

'HOW can I make my dialogue like real-life conversation?' The cry goes up whenever three or more would-be writers are gathered together. (The collective noun for any gathering of writers of potential best-sellers is, of course, a scribble of pens.)

The answer to that one is – you don't *want* your dialogue to sound like real-life conversation, which, you will have noticed, if you have a keen ear, is full of ums and ers, half-finished sentences, coughs, interruptions, and unnecessary pauses. The importance of interrupted dialogue, to serve a specific purpose, will be discussed later. Right now what we are talking about is the conversations that take place between the main characters, or those of the hero or heroine with one or more minor characters, to advance the book.

You can get more points across in dialogue than you can in narrative, and you should. Conversation is the sparkle in the champagne, without it a book would be very flat wine indeed; in fact it wouldn't be a book at all. Life is full of conversation – or was until television came along – and while the kind of banal chit-chat you'll hear in the queue at the supermarket check-out bears little relation to the sparkling exchanges between two conflicting people in a book, it wouldn't do you any harm to eavesdrop on the chit-chat occasionally. At least you'll learn what to avoid if nothing else.

In plays and films everyone speaks their lines with a certain panache. They have something to say – put in their mouths by scriptwriter or playwright needless to say – and on their ability as actors/actresses rests the success and impact on our, the audience's ears. I recently went to a Tom Stoppard play, *Jumpers*, with Tom Courtenay and Julie Walters. The plot wouldn't bear inspection under a microscope, but oh, to hear Tom Courtenay philosophising was a joy. He had a bewitched audience, I promise you. Now, your words are going into cold print, it won't be Burt Reynolds or Paul Newman delivering them, so you have to make them all the better. Your reader is going to have to see the hero and heroine in her mind's eye as she reads, and never underestimate the power of your reader's imagination. As a little girl (a very wise and intelligent little girl) once remarked, when asked why she preferred radio plays to those on television: 'The scenery's much better.' So it is.

So you want to know how to make the conversational exchanges between your characters crackle with a life of their own, and you want them to have consistency with their own personalities. If your hero is a powerful character, as he has to be, let's face it, then there is no way he is going to dither about, either in conversation or actions. His words will be as forceful as he is. Similarly, if your heroine is a strong-willed gal with a mind of her own, she will respond in like manner.

Let's analyse the first few pages of a book called *Daughter of the Sun*. The heroine is Charlotte Breck, who, determined to find her lost explorer father in Peru, has the opportunity to do so when she hears that Gil Bryden is mounting an archaeological expedition to find a lost city there. Charlotte's uncle is also in the party, which is how she knows about it. She goes to Peru, not aware yet that the said Gil Bryden, because of her nickname, 'Charlie', thinks she is a man, determined to persuade him to take her with the expedition. The book starts with Charlotte's arrival at the primitive airport somewhere in Peru. She expects her uncle to meet her, but instead is met by Gil Bryden.

Now the setting is firmly in your mind, but not yet in your reader's, for what is going to be a confrontation that will set the scene for future exchanges. It is essential, especially at the beginning, that the dialogue and narrative are interspersed so that the reader is informed *painlessly* of both setting and circumstances. (Note: readers do not like huge chunks of descriptive matter. They skip them. Then they have to go back, because they've missed some small but vital piece of information in the bits they skipped, and they get annoyed and probably won't buy your next book, and serve you right.)

Daughter of the Sun

Sypnopsis

'You'll just have to go back to England. I don't want you here.' The man looked down at Charlotte Breck as he spoke. His eyes were hard and devoid of expression.

Three things are established in these first few lines: 1. The setting is somewhere abroad. 2. The hero is definitely unfriendly and certainly tough. 3. He's taller!

His whole face said it for him instead. She thought she had never met such a rude, arrogant man in all her life. And if he thought she was going meekly to accept his startling words, he was in for a shock! She smiled at him.

But the heroine (Charlotte) is about to fight back. Has he met his match? Read on to find out …

'No, I won't,' she said. 'I don't care whether you want me or not. I'm here to stay. Now are you going to take me to the hotel to see my uncle, or do I call a taxi?'

There's an uncle somewhere in the background.

'Taxi? Hotel?' He began to laugh. 'Good grief, woman, where the hell do you think you are? London?'

His scorn for her ignorance shows he's aggressive as well as unfriendly.

Charlotte held on to her temper – with some difficulty. The dark auburn hair tumbling down her shoulders was a good indication of her temperament.

Auburn hair and a temper to match. Ouch!

'All right,' she said sweetly,

She's fighting back with a touch of

hiding the smoulder well, 'so I've made a funny. Let's all have a good laugh, shall we — and then go?'

sweet sarcasm — he's not going to like that, is he?

Gil Bryden took a long slow look at her. The gaze started at the top of her head, worked its way down at leisurely pace, and finished at her toes. Then he looked into her eyes again. His were flint, with perhaps a touch of steel. She looked back unflinchingly.

Sparks about to fly any minute now.

'Well?' she said.
'Charlie,' he answered. 'My God — Charlie. I expected a man — and I get you!'

We now know that he expected a man, Charlie, not a woman, Charlotte. We'll find out why later on.

It was getting more difficult by the moment to resist the urge to punch him right on the jaw. Charlotte wondered if she'd make it.

Charlotte is holding on to her temper but only just.

'And as you can see,' she said grittily, 'I'm not a man. Well done — ten out of ten for observation. You should also be able to see, if you weren't so busy giving me steely glances, that everyone is staring at us, no doubt expecting us to have a fight at any moment —'

She can be nearly as aggressive as he is.

'Damn them,' he observed, and looked round casually at the knots of people standing nearby on the tarmac with fascinated expressions. There

His reaction, and that of the onlookers, reveals more of his personality.

was an immediate shifting of gazes, as if his manner was sufficiently threatening in itself, and then movement, as the small groups dispersed towards the airport buildings.

He looked back at Charlotte. 'They just lost interest,' he remarked.

He also has a dry wit.

'I'm not surprised,' she said dryly. 'What's your speciality? Killing people at ten paces with a glance?'

So does she. The conflict is well established now.

'No. Sending superfluous females back from whence they came, in double quick time. What's yours?'

Swift retort from Gil ...

'Keeping my temper intact in the face of sheer male chauvinist piggery,' she responded smartly.

Followed by one equally swift from Charlotte.

'Hmm, and lippy too. You endear yourself to me more with every second that passes, Charlie —'

Now it's his turn for sarcasm.

'Charlotte,' she snapped.

Just reminding him of her name. Which doesn't do much good ...

'Charlie,' he went on as if he hadn't heard. 'But it doesn't make a scrap of difference. The jungle is no place for a woman —'

At last we know that they are near jungle ...

'Fiddlesticks! Where've you been living for the past forty years? A monastery? The

And that she is a liberated woman ...

world's advanced a little since
you were born –'

'Thirty-five,' he corrected.   *And his age is thirty-five …*
'And not a monastery –'

'I can cope anywhere,' she cut   *And now she's letting him know*
in. He wasn't the only one   *that she is tougher than him (or so*
who could interrupt. 'Prob-   *she thinks).*
ably better than you. Women
are born tougher than men –'

'You're nuts!' he glared down   *Charlotte is feeling the strain*
at her, eyes glinting with   *now …*
something Charlotte wasn't
too sure about. It could have
been anger, it could equally
well have been derision. She
wasn't sure which she preferred. She knew one thing –
she was extremely hot, and
thirsty.

'And you're very rude. I'm   *But still fighting.*
dying for a long cool drink,
and I'm fed up with standing
here entertaining dozens of
natives, so –'

'All right, we'll go and get a   *Here he shows mercy and carries*
drink. And we'll talk.' He   *her cases. Perhaps he has a heart,*
picked up her two suitcases and   *somewhere.*
swung away with them,
leaving her to follow.

'There's nothing more to talk   *Obviously he has long strides! A*
about,' she said breathlessly,   *description of building, but sketched*
catching up with him as he   *in lightly.*
reached the rickety white
wooden building.

'That's what you think.' He   *Quite a lot of everything here. A* spared her a glance as he dumped her cases unceremoniously on the baked-earth floor by a table. 'Sit down. I'll be back in a minute,' and he strode away. Charlotte looked around her. She'd arrived. She was here. The welcome had been, to put it at its mildest, not quite what she had expected, but she'd made it. And nothing, but nothing, was going to put her off now. Especially not an aggressive, black-haired, six-foot-five hunk of ill-mannered manhood called Gil Bryden. Then she remembered the gypsy fortune-teller's words, and caught her breath – and quickly erased the thought from her mind as she saw him returning. Later. She would think about that later.

more detailed description of Gil, impression of heat of place (baked-earth floor). And a clue – gypsy – that will be explained later, leaving just a touch of mystery for now.

He sat down opposite her and pushed a cup of steaming liquid over to her. 'Coffee,' he said. 'At least the water's boiled. Cold drinks are highly suspect here, until you're used to the bugs.' He sipped his cool-looking lime-green drink with an expression that barely escaped being a smirk.

He's started to put the boot in here, making her feel unsure of their surroundings – there's more to come!

'I've had all my shots,' she answered, gazing in dismay at the dark brown coffee. It looked awful.

She would like to pull a face here, but doesn't.

'Hmm? Fascinating. I didn't know they'd invented one to cope with Montezuma's Revenge yet.' He glanced at the watch on his tanned wrist. 'Nearly noon. I advise you to drink up. The insect world hereabouts comes to life any time. Mosquitoes, flies – you name it, we've got it. We've also got snakes.'

Gil is really putting the pressure on now.

'You mean they just fly in at the window? How interesting. I've never seen flying snakes before,' she responded, all wide-eyed innocence.

Quick-witted retort by our game heroine.

'Have your little joke. I mean where we – that is, your uncle, myself, and a few assorted bearers – are going –'

He's letting her know she's not going with them. Subtly!

'And me.'

Two words pregnant with meaning!

There was a dreadful, brief silence. There was a difference now. They weren't standing out in the baking sun, with him towering over her. They were almost on eye-level terms, sitting across from each other at a rickety wooden table in a building that was scarcely any cooler. People milled about in the near distance, voices echoed, and it all washed round them as they sat there in an oasis of mutual antipathy. Charlotte's eyes met

Narrative, descriptions of him and of the place, essential, establishing atmosphere.

the man's, and she saw his face clearly, and watched it. Hard, square stubborn-chinned, shaggy black hair, deep-tanned features, wide mouth, straight nose, thick dark eyebrows over those hostile eyes that watched her.

'No,' he said. She wondered if he ever smiled. Perhaps he had no teeth — maybe, she thought hopefully, someone knocked them out for him, and he's ashamed. It made her feel a little brighter anyway. And direct confrontation with a man like that would solve nothing.

The tension leavened with some humour.

Charlotte, brain working in top gear, decided to try another tactic. After all, he was hardly going to frogmarch her back to the nearest plane and force her aboard.

She's fighting back. Brave girl!

She sighed gently. It was really rather a good sigh, so she repeated it. 'I'm looking forward to seeing Uncle Max,' she said. 'I thought he'd be here to meet me,' she even managed to put a little catch in her voice.

Pulling out all the stops.

At that he smiled. She was a little disappointed to see that not only did he appear to have the full complement of teeth, but that they were good, white

Touch more description to complete picture of Gil.

– and as strong-looking as the rest of him.

'That's better.' He tapped her cup. 'Drink up. Max had a touch of fever – nothing to worry about, but I advised him to rest up today.'

Slight relaxing of tension, before he socks it to her again.

'I see.' She swallowed a grimace. The coffee was the bitterest she had ever tasted. Surprisingly though, it made her feel a little better. She drank some more.

That coffee tastes terrible, doesn't it?

'Like it?' he asked. As if he cared!

He's polite, but wait for it …

'It's – a little strong, but – um – quite nice,' she said cautiously.

She is, rightly, on her guard.

'It gets worse – out in the jungle, I mean,' he said in conversational tones. 'I'd hardly dare to begin to tell you about all the difficulties in the simple business of keeping alive –'

Now the attack.

'My father told me when I was a child,' said Charlotte gently. She was going to enjoy this. She was going to watch his face very carefully when she said what she had to say next. 'Or didn't Uncle Max tell you that his brother-in-law was Guy Breck?'

But she's ready for it and socks it to him, and how.

'My God!' She knew. She had known that Uncle Max

More explanation of relationship with uncle and her father – and in wouldn't have mentioned the relationship, because he and Guy had quarrelled years ago, and never spoken afterwards.

a moment we'll know why he's surprised.

Gil looked hard at her. 'Your father was Guy Breck?'

His reaction. Stunned, to say the least.

She lifted her chin. 'Yes.'

A simple answer.

'I met him, after his expedition up the Amazon, about twelve years ago. But Max never —'

More explanations, letting us see he's a much-travelled man.

'No, he wouldn't. They didn't speak. It was a —' she shrugged — 'a stupid quarrel — a family matter. I'd like to see my uncle,' she said gently.

Family squabbles.

Gil Bryden wasn't exactly shaken, she could tell that. It would take something equivalent to an earthquake to do more than raise his eyebrows, but at least she'd had the satisfaction of seeing him momentarily lost for words. And it was enough — for now.

Charlotte is satisfied with his reaction ...

He stood up, looked down at her now empty coffee cup, and then at her. 'If you want to see your uncle, we'd better go,' he said. 'I have a car outside.' Charlotte rose to her feet, the momentary feeling of triumph evaporating in the intense heat. She mustn't let him see that she was at all affected by it. That would never do. And she

But is having a struggle with the intense heat.

would soon get acclimatised anyway.

He led the way out into the heat of the noonday sun, and Charlotte followed. The land was flat around them, shimmering faintly, almost seeming to vibrate. In the distance – she turned to look – were the mountains, and the jungle, dark and mysterious trees, and mountains of eternal mystery. She felt her heartbeats quicken. Here! She was here at last, and nothing was going to stop her.

Background description.

She became aware that he was watching her, that he had reached a car, and stood holding the door open, waiting for her. 'Take a good look,' he said sardonically.

He is not letting up the pressure.

She turned and looked at the car. It was an old battered vehicle that seemed as if it would disintegrate if anyone tried to move it.

But wait for it …

'At the car?' she enquired. 'Hmm – well, it has seen better days, I suppose, but what would you like me to say about it?' and she gave him a sweet smile.

She won't be beaten by him. Deliberate misunderstanding on her part.

'Not the car – the scenery.'

He explains. Patiently, we feel.

'Oh, I see. It's much as I expected. I did read up on Peru, you know – and my

More attack. But can he be weakening?

father told me a lot.' She slid in. The cracked leather upholstery burned like fire through her thin cotton dress, but she gave no indication. Gil Bryden slammed her door, and she winced, but it held. Then he was in beside her. He turned towards her. 'You can't stay, you know,' he said conversationally. 'You must see that it's impossible –'

'No, I don't, as a matter of fact.' Her eyes were green, and she could make them very cold when she chose. 'What's impossible about it?'

Resistance from Charlotte.

'You couldn't cope for a –'

Attack from Gil again.

'How do you know?' Fire lit her face. 'How do you know what I can do? I might be better than you –'

And Charlotte fights back well.

'At living in the jungle? Constantly watching out for snakes – crossing rivers with alligators waiting to snap your legs off – climbing up to where the air is so thin it takes all the strength from –'

Gil is really on the attack now.

'Try me,' she snapped. She held up her hand, a gold bangle encircling her slim wrist. 'Take my hand. Grip it as hard as you like. Go on.'

A challenge from Charlotte. (Foolish girl!)

The corner of his mouth twitched. 'Don't be an idiot.

The strong male, amused by a weak woman.

You're not seriously suggesting you pit your strength against mine —'

'I just asked you to do something. What's the matter? Scared?'

Charlotte needling him.

He silently held up his hand and gripped hers. 'Now what?' he seemed almost amused — humouring a precocious child.

Gil humouring her …

'Now try and pull my hand towards you,' she said.

Silly girl …

She felt the tensing of his muscles, the gradual power as his hand tightened over hers. Charlotte braced herself to resist the pull.

She loses, naturally.

She knew what he would do. He would try a sudden jerk, and she was prepared for it. But he didn't. He looked at her, and slowly, gradually, she felt her hand being drawn irresistibly towards him. Now. Now. She jerked her hand with all her strength, felt a second of triumph — and then it was all over. Her hand lay against his chest, imprisoned, helpless. Slowly then he released her.

'Satisfied?' he mocked.

He rubs in the fact, the beast.

She pulled her hand free. 'You cheated!' she gasped.

She's still trying …

'No, I didn't. I did what you

Concessions made, but only slightly.

asked. So? Okay, you're strong. Is that what you want me to say? But you need more. You need stamina — and sheer guts, and a determination to survive anything.'

'I have it. I have it,' she declared.   *Her determination shows.*

He said nothing, merely turned away, and started the engine, which juddered and shook in violent protest. 'Hold on,' he said, unnecessarily. Charlotte had no intention of doing otherwise. She was still smouldering from his cavalier treatment. How on earth did he and Uncle Max manage to get on without coming to blows?

She is now furious with him.

Max Temple had a temperament as fiery as Charlotte's, with the red hair to go with it. And this man — she took a breath as they hit a pothole in the unmade track, and landed with a thud — this man was as prickly and aggressive as a wounded lion.

Descriptions of uncle — and road — and more of Gil.

The track widened, and shacks appeared, surrounded by trees, and a few Indians watched them pass with little interest. The heat haze filled the car, and Gil Bryden swerved to avoid two scrawny hens scratching and pecking at some-

More background.

thing in the middle of the road.
Road! Charlotte thought.

'Just a couple of miles further,' he shouted above the appalling noise of the engine. Charlotte didn't answer. She was busy thinking, and working out her plans. She didn't see him glance briefly at her, nor the expression in his eyes. It was perhaps just as well.

A hint of mystery here. What was that expression in his eyes? We'll find out later of course, but for now the reader is kept on tenterhooks (hopefully).

And that's it. An analysis of the first eight pages of a romantic novel that has been translated into many languages and sold all over the world. I hope not Peru, because I've never been there, and the Peruvian reader might just find a couple of minor inaccuracies, and, oh, didn't I mention? It's one of mine. Book nineteen, I think, written in 1977 before it was fashionable for hero and heroine to go to bed together, and they don't. (See Chapter 10, 'Beyond The Bedroom Door'.)

The relationship and the conflict are established in those first few pages, and it continues pretty much all the way through, interspersed with tender passages, danger, and a few dozen other ploys designed to keep the reader actually reading.

The greater sense of conflict comes across in the dialogue, the sparking interchanges which begin with Gil's first words to Charlotte when she has just stepped off a plane and is clearly suffering from jet-lag. The pressure he exerts on her continues for a long time into the book. Until … no, you'll just have to read it to find out, won't you?

To summarise then. Dialogue helps to advance the action and the reader to know the characters more fully. Some writers find it easy, to others it is extremely difficult. To the latter I would advise reading out loud to hear how it sounds – or persuading someone else to read it for you. You'll hear it more objectively that way. If it sounds stilted to you it will certainly come over to the reader in the same way, thus stopping the easy flow of her reading. Listen to plays, particularly on radio – and learn from those. But perhaps the most important thing of all is to *know* your characters thoroughly before you begin to write the book, for if you do, they will speak for themselves, and you will be merely the observer, listening in and writing down what they have to say.

'I say, Mary, hold on a minute, didn't you –'

'Didn't I what?'

'Didn't you mention something about –'

'Get to the point, for heaven's sake. Mention something about –'

'If you'd let me *finish* a sentence you might find out.'

'Oh, all right. Finish your sentence. Honestly! Some people –'

'You said you'd tell us about interrupted dialogue.'

'Oh. That. You mean when people start to say something, and –'

'Someone else finishes the sentence for them? Yes, I suppose that's what I –'

'Well, why didn't you say so at the beginning?'

'I tried to only you kept interrupting me. There, I've said it.'

'Ah. Well, basically it's interesting to use occasionally, as for example, when your hero and heroine are having, let's say an argument or –'

'Or a serious discussion?'

'Yes, I suppose so. You see it helps to –'

'Advance the plot?'

'Yes. Will you let me finish?'

'Oops. Sorry, Mary. Only I'm just beginning to see what you –'

'Mean? Oh. Good. Is that it, then? I mean, does that answer all your –'

'Well, almost. There was one other teensy thing – er –'

'Yes?'

'Well, do you need to put "he saids" and "she saids" in these passages of interrupted dialogue?'

'No. It should be evident from the conversation. If you do feel the need, you could occasionally add "he said in exasperation", or "she glared as she said it" but you don't need to because it is only for a brief time, say half a page at most. Otherwise it would become –'

'Tedious?'

'Mmm. Precisely. I'm going now. I have to start the next chapter. So I'll just say –'

'Right! I can take a hint. Goodbye!'

NINE

Caution – Writers At Work

YOU probably imagine a romantic novelist sitting at a desk looking out over an expanse of flowers in the garden, while a gentle breeze caresses the trees, as she pauses, pen in hand, and waits for the muse to visit her, don't you? And she is, of course, clad in a mauve tea-gown or something similar, and there is a vase of sweet-scented roses on the table nearby, from which, every so often, a petal will fall gently on to the polished table, and she will give a sigh of contentment and put pen to paper ... that's what I used to think romantic novelists did too, once upon a time in the long ago before I started to write them.

In fact, I also cherished a vague idea that *all* novelists lived somewhere in the South of France or Monte Carlo, say, in a white villa overlooking the waters of the Mediterranean, with yachts bobbing gently at anchor while from the distant casinos came the click of the roulette wheel. Ah, dreams.

The house where I live and have my being and do my writing is occupied by the following, variously and frequently all at once: a husband, Derek, a twenty-year-old daughter, Judith, a teenaged son, David, a large eating machine known as a black labrador, named Minty, an even larger moving hearthrug on four legs called Muffin who acquired us one Boxing Day, three cats, three goldfish and assorted stray animals that appear from time to time and have to be fed before a search goes up for good homes.

And in the midst of this chaos, I write. I write because: a) I have to, and b) because I'm not brilliantly good at anything else and it's the perfect excuse for not giving dinner parties or going to coffee mornings.

I handed a questionnaire to thirty or so of my writer friends (all romantic or would-be romantic novelists) and one of the questions was: 'Are you a compulsive writer?' And back came all the forms with a resounding: Yes! (often underlined). Don't worry, you are not going to get a lot of statistics on the lines of 87 per cent said yes to the question 'Do you ever get a writing block?' Because I never understand statistics anyway, and suspect that nobody else does either, and they are also extremely boring. But yes, most of them do experience that awful hopeless feeling of not being able to write another word; the solutions they gave to this were many and varied, including getting out of the house for a day or two, doing belated spring cleaning (enough to make anyone want to get back to writing), to reading, reading and even more reading; and one practical person even answered that she sat and wrote anything that came into her head, even to the extent of making a Christmas card list in July so as simply to be involved in the physical act of writing. I would also add that talking to a fellow writer, in person or on the telephone, is a great help.

I learned long, long ago that writers are not like other people. We see the world differently, we respond differently to things that happen. We *are* different. If I had known that when I was a child, it would have made life a lot easier. I was never part of the pack, either at school or play, never the first to be chosen when teams were being made up for school or party games. I used to wonder vaguely why. When I went to an old girls' reunion a year ago, I discovered the reason, after all those years. A classmate from aeons ago said, 'You always seemed to be not entirely with us.' No, she didn't mean I was dotty, or at least I hope not! She only confirmed what it had said on all my school reports, which were so horrendous that I always used to hide them in the hopes (vain) that my parents would forget. 'Mary is always day-dreaming' – 'Mary is lazy' – 'Mary must try harder'. Mary didn't want to try harder, Mary only wanted to write (and did) short stories, plays, westerns and poems. And in the years since then, talking over schooldays with many other writers, it has been the same story repeated over and over again.

So if you are a teacher and you have a day-dreamer in your class who the others regard as odd, cultivate her because one day she will probably write best-sellers.

'Why do you write?' was another question I asked. The most devastatingly simple answer of all summed it up: 'Because I must.' I also asked, 'What would you be if you were not a writer?' Various replies came to that: an artist, a bookseller, a librarian, an actress, Tarzan's mate(!), or quite simply: 'Miserable!' If I were not a writer I'd love to be a wild-life photographer but I would probably write a book about my travels, so I would still be a writer. There's no escape.

All those who answered the questionnaire had a strict routine of writing daily for several hours, starting at various times but generally between nine and ten in the morning. One or two found they could often continue writing late at night when a book was going well, but that was extra to their daily stint. The would-be writers who answered the questionnaire mostly had other jobs or young children to look after, and therefore had to be more flexible in their hours, but I was pleasantly surprised to find that *all* were determined to find time every day.

I am always fascinated to read of the lives of other writers, and a large part of the books in my study are by writers telling of their lives, how they came to be writers, methods of working, etc. Paul Gallico's *Confessions of a Story Teller* is one of the earliest I bought. Monica Dickens' autobiography, *An Open Door*, is a joy to read, as are all her books. And I have many more. So why don't I interview fellow writers, I thought? Find out what makes them tick, because, in spite of the basic rules of writing, everyone is unique. The results of my interviews fascinated me. I hope you will find them equally informative. Not all the women I spoke to wrote for Mills & Boon, and some wrote only historical romances, but all have one thing in common. The compulsion to write.

I combined a visit to Stratford-on-Avon to see *Richard III* with my first interview, which was with Jane Donnelly, one of Mills & Boon's favourite authors — and one of mine. I have read and enjoyed all her books and keep them in the bookcase in the guest bedroom for visitors to read.

Jane began writing for Mills & Boon sixteen years ago, but before that had written many thrillers and westerns under different names. She told me that it is essential for her to write every day, to keep the thread of continuity going, and she writes by hand or using a typewriter – of which, I might add, she has several dotted all over the house, so that she is never far away from one! She works better in the morning, is totally hooked on writing, and carries a small portable tape-recorder with her whenever she leaves home in case ideas strike. And while those ideas can come from anywhere at all, she finds that pictures are a big help to her, and when researching the setting for her books, takes a lot of photographs of the places which she then sticks on a board in her study for reference.

'I'm a compulsive writer,' she said. 'I write all the time, and when I get ideas, I jot them down on the backs of menus, cigarette packets, chequebooks – anything that's to hand. I also keep a tape-recorder by the side of my bed in case inspiration strikes in the middle of the night.' She added, 'I always read my dialogue into the tape-recorder to hear how it sounds.'

Her heroines are all intelligent young women with minds of their own; the books are optimistic in outlook. 'I like to leave the reader with the impression that the future is bright,' she added, and then told me that she goes around with the next book forming in her head before even beginning, and that it's lovely to take 'bits and bobs' of people she knows for characters.

Sheila Walsh was next on my list. She has been writing since 1975, when she won the Netta Muskett Award from the Romantic Novelists' Association for her first book *The Golden Songbird*, which was accepted by Hurst & Blackett. She has now written twelve, the latest of which is *A Highly Respectable Marriage* which won her the Romantic Novelists Association's Major Award, and is being brought out by Mills & Boon Harlequin. Her books are historical romances, published not only in the United Kingdom but in America, by New American Library. Her first book came about almost by accident, she told me. She was (and still is) a member of the Southport Writers' Circle, and had taken a first chapter of a book along to a manuscript evening – where it was greeted with such enthusiasm that she decided she might as well finish it! As good a reason as any for writing a book. 'I have a mental filing cabinet, to which I add ideas,' she told me. 'I don't write them down, just keep adding, until one day the mixture is bubbling over and I have to do something physical about it, namely, beginning a book. I write in the mornings, generally, and other times if at all possible and if the book is going well. I never plan in advance, and sit down every morning not knowing what is going to happen. I "know" all my characters in my head before I begin, and if they are right, the plot evolves naturally.' Until recently she wrote her books in longhand, but has now trained herself to think directly onto a typewriter. 'Where do I get my ideas from? Anywhere and everywhere. A germ of an idea, something I've seen or read – like the grit in the oyster, it grows and takes shape until characters begin to emerge and come to life, and then it's all systems go!'

My next interviewee is also a highly successful writer for Mills & Boon. Anne Thomas was a journalist before she became a romantic novelist. She began writing for Mills & Boon in 1975 under the pseudonym Sara Craven, and has now written nearly thirty. 'I decided at the age of four that I was a writer and wrote my first novel, *Arcade of Light*, which, alas, I never finished. I wasn't even sure what arcade meant, which seemed totally unimportant! I've always loved words. I played in the garden when I was a child, lived in a fantasy world, acted the fantasies out, and wrote plays and stories. History fascinated me. I still have a secret yearning to write a historical romance and I'm sure I will soon.' She went on: 'I work office hours, 10 a.m. to 4 p.m. – and occasionally break the rules and take a day off, which is a deliciously guilty feeling! I would write even if I were not published, simply because I am, and have always been, a compulsive writer.'

I asked her about her working methods. 'I think onto a typewriter, thanks to my journalistic training,' she told me, 'and walk round the house acting out pieces of dialogue – which has been known to give the window cleaner the shock of his life! I like music when I'm writing, hard rock, played very loudly. If I'm very pleased with a scene I may even dance – or cry!'

'Ideas?' I asked. 'Can you give me any examples of how a book comes into being?'

'Oh, yes,' she answered. 'Just recently I came down from my study in mid-afternoon to watch an old Dirk Bogarde movie on

TV, *Ill Met By Moonlight*. I had seen it ages before and couldn't remember why it had made such a strong impression on me. The moment the theme music began, I remembered. It had been that haunting music by Mikis Theodorakis which had had that strange effect – and immediately, almost like a film unrolling in my mind, came an entire plot for a book, *Alien Vengeance*, which I wrote straightaway. I often get titles first, which is a great help, and one of my most successful books was triggered off by reading a Sunday colour supplement about emerald smuggling in Colombia. From that article came *Flame of Diablo*.' She smiled and added: 'Just one more thing to tell your readers. I hope to continue writing till I'm ninety-three!' I'm sure she will.

I had to travel north of the border for my next interview, with Alanna Knight. I love Scottish settings for my books, so was able to combine some research with the trip. Alanna lives in Aberdeen with her husband Alastair, and has two grown-up sons. She had her first modern gothic novel published in 1969, *Legend of the Loch*, which won her the Romantic Novelists' Assocation's Netta Muskett award. Since then she has written twenty novels, several of them for Mills & Boon Masquerade series under the name Margaret Hope. Alanna has also written *The Robert Louis Stevenson Treasury* (to be published in late 1985), a most impressive and comprehensively researched book about that writer – which took her four years to write.

She is a full-time writer and told me: 'I became the reluctant possessor of a word processor last year. It was like a Mills & Boon romance. Initial attraction, then hatred and conflict, and now I wonder how I ever lived without it!'

As she cannot – and does not even intend to – think onto either the word processor or a typewriter, she writes all her books in longhand, using pencil, into a lined notebook which has to be the same size each time. 'The big moment of each day,' she said, 'is the sharpening of the four pencils I keep on my desk, and then I'm away. I write from 9 a.m. to 1 p.m. daily and keep my afternoons free for strictly non-creative activities: housework, cooking, visiting friends or shopping. Then in the evening I often begin writing again, perhaps round about 9 o'clock, and also do any editing and preparation for the following morning's work.'

I asked her the old question everyone wants answered: 'Where do you get your ideas from?' 'Ideas,' she replied, 'come in all shapes or sizes — usually human. I can visit a place, and that triggers off a person, either modern or historical. I start to see him or her distantly at first but growing clearer all the time. At that delicate stage I don't probe too hard. I'm perfectly happy for them to take up residence in my mind for a little while until they are perfectly formed and ready to be born.'

She enjoys classical music and usually has some playing in the background whilst writing. She told me that she always carries a notebook with her wherever she goes and would feel naked without it. On this she jots down dialogue, ideas, etc. She is, she added, a compulsive writer, always has been and always will be.

A writers' conference in Scarborough was the setting for my next three interviews. I was lucky to catch the first — as you will understand when you read what followed.

I don't really know where to begin with Jean Saunders (alias Jean Innes, Rowena Summers, Sally Blake!). Before she started writing romantic novels she published over six hundred short stories here and abroad! As if that's not enough she has now added to that score forty romantic novels, under four different names, with several different publishers. And as if *that*'s not enough, she lectures at various writers' conferences, women's groups and schools. Oh yes, she's also married with three grown-up children!

She told me: 'I have always been a compulsive writer, and began seriously when my children were at junior school. I taught myself to type, wrote my first short stories longhand then typed them out, but gradually learnt to think straight onto a typewriter, which made it so much easier for me.' She works regular office hours, all day, every day, and has her own study which is completely shut off from all interruptions.

'I hear my characters' voices in my head as I write — and then the dialogue is as *they* would say it, not as the author (me!) would. I write both modern and historical romances, and for the latter do enormous amounts of research, sometimes borrowing as many as twenty books from the library for one. Most writers get their characters first, but I work on the assumption that a man and woman are going to be the principal characters anyway, therefore I prefer to find my setting first.' She gave me an example of this with the following gem of information; 'I'm researching the Indian Mutiny at the moment for a book to be called *Burnished Land*. This dictates the role of my characters. The heroine is the daughter of an officer in the East India Company, and the hero, a Scotsman, is a descendant of characters in a previous book, *Scarlet Rebel*, which is giving me a glorious sense of continuity from the past.

'When I'm researching Rowena Summers books, which are now all set in the West Country, I visit the locations and get as much local colour as I can. As I live in the West Country myself I feel I bring a special empathy to these books. As well as a passionate love story, I think readers like to learn a little bit about the area in which books are set.' She looked at her watch then, said, 'Sorry, must dash, I'm giving a lecture in five minutes.' There's energy for you. Next time we meet I'm going to ask what vitamins she takes!

The next writer I interviewed was Catherine Fellows who won the Netta Muskett award in 1971 with her first historical romance, *Leonora*, which was published by Hurst & Blackett after being serialised in *Woman's Own*. This book and the following five have all sold in the USA as well as in Britain. 'I started writing pony stories at the age of eleven because I have always loved horses,' she told me. 'Unfortunately I never finished them! I wrote purely for my own entertainment because I had the compulsion to write, and still do, although I take a great deal longer than many of my contemporaries, and do a fair amount of rewriting.'

I asked her if she thought directly onto a typewriter; she answered, 'Not until the age of seventeen when I taught myself to type on a machine so ancient that it really should have had "Patent Applied For" stamped on it. Now I use a word processor but still think fondly of that first typewriter.'

She added, 'When I wrote *Leonora*, it was in a way as a defence against a house full of children (seven in all!) and I could lose myself in the Regency period whilst all about me was chaos. I had started it when I was eighteen originally, never finished it, but had been haunted by it ever since. The opening paragraph of the book came from a school essay I had written at fifteen.

'Now that the children are all grown up, I generally begin writing in the morning around 10 o'clock, continue through the day (with various interruptions from my two dogs) and, occasionally, if a book is going really well, start again late in the evening. The ideas for my books come out of thin air – when I'm doing very mundane tasks such as ironing or peeling sprouts. Two books came to me simply as a result of an opening sentence. One was: "I won't marry him, I don't care what you say." That was all, just those ten words which had popped into my head whilst gardening. I hadn't a clue what they meant, so had to write the book in order to find out. That was *The Marriage Masque*. All my books have been set in the Regency period but I'm now branching out into moderns, and have had two accepted by Mills & Boon. I'm really enjoying the change.'

My next interview was with Julia Fitzgerald who has been writing since the age of six, when she wrote her first short stories. She wrote her first full-length novel at seventeen, since when she has written thirty-two more, all best-sellers, and all but two historical. 'I write best in the evening,' she said, 'which was very difficult when my children were smaller, and I was alone with them, but I coped.' She went on, 'I have always been a compulsive writer – isn't everybody? – and taught myself to type. I also taped two books but although I found that method, dictating onto tape, easier, the books were more reflective, which slowed the action – which in turn didn't suit my editor who persuaded me to return to typing! I now have a word processor and have "settled down" with it so that I can write a complete chapter from brain to paper in two hours.

'I do lots of extensive research all the time – even in my sleep.'

Of course I asked her the old old question: 'Where do you get your ideas from?' I've had it asked me so many times I decided to get my own back on someone else, and chose Julia. Her answer came back so swiftly that I decided she must be a mind reader. 'Ideas?' she echoed. 'From everything and everywhere; one sentence in a film, or poem or book. Music also stirs me and inspires me, and I always play it when writing. It's rich with inspiration. I use colour to stimulate my imagination as well. Favourite? Rich blue, with which I surround myself in furnishings, clothes, pictures, etcetera. I've written two books with the theme Arabian belly-dancing – and practise that too ... in privacy I hasten to add! It's marvellous exercise, which is a bonus because I believe that regular exercise (i.e. cycling to the shops) is essential to the creative force. Diet is also very important, and I also meditate and practise auto-hypnosis.'

I interviewed my next writer, Aileen Armitage (who has also written under the name Aileen Quigley), at the weekend writers' conference in Scarborough. She has been writing since 1967 and had her first book, *King's Pawn*, published in 1970. Since that time she has written nineteen more, including two modern romances. Before then she was a teacher but her sight failed, and she is now registered blind. Her courage and tenacity are therefore all the more admirable. She told me: 'Nothing is going to stop me writing. After I left teaching, I was at home with my four children, and I was absolutely determined to write. I had always written – school magazines, college papers, and that kind of thing – but now I decided it was going to be a book. I began at first writing in longhand, using thick felt-tipped pens on jotters, which I then sent to a typist. Now I have learned to touch type, and I'm planning to buy a word processor, which will make work more straightforward.'

She went on: 'My biggest problem, being a historical novelist, is having to cope with the vast quantities of research material I need. I used to persuade my children to read to me but now I use a closed-circuit camera mounted above my desk and pointed down at the book I wish to read. The image is projected onto a large display screen which can magnify print to make the letters enormous – one foot high if necessary! – and I have learnt to manage very well.'

She added that the best writing time for her is between six in the evening and 2 a.m. 'It is self-discipline and sheer determination that are most important,' she announced firmly, with which viewpoint I agree whole-heartedly. Her cheerful attitude came across to me as strongly as her determination, and when she added casually, 'I also lecture on novels, and travel all over the country to various writers' conferences,' I was no longer surprised. She is possessed of boundless energy and good humour. I don't need to add that she is a compulsive writer, do I?

I've known my next interviewee since 1970, when she and I joined a writers' circle in Manchester as two very shy newcomers, discovered very swiftly that not a lot of writing was actually ever done by the majority of the other members, and in a matter of months had reorganised the set-up. I'm sure they were glad to see us leave! We've been firm friends ever since, and it was she I used to phone in tears when yet another manuscript came thudding through the letter box. She insists that it was I who nagged her into writing her first book, and yes, she's right, I did. Her name is Eileen Jackson.

She was first published in 1976, since when she has written seven historical romances, three moderns, and has one modern and two historicals in the pipeline.

I asked her why she wrote. 'I can't remember ever wanting to do anything else,' she answered with faint surprise. 'I used to make little theatres out of cardboard boxes when I was very young, and would act out very gruesome plays for myself and sister when we went to bed. We're both over fifty now, but she still blames me for being afraid of the dark!' She had her first story published at the age of nine. 'I'd written a romantic tale,' she explained, 'and hidden it away, but an aunt found it and sent it off. A man from the newspaper came to interview me and demanded to know where I'd copied it from, which annoyed me greatly because it was all my own work.' She continued writing – and reading, anything and everything – until at the age of thirty-nine she decided, 'It was now or never. I thought, if I'm not published by the time I'm forty, I'll give up. Almost immediately afterwards I began to sell my short stories. The biggest thrill in my life was receiving £10 from the *Sunday Post* for one!'

She and her husband collect ephemera – ancient newspapers and books – which she uses for source material. She has always loved history and her first book *Lord Rivington's Lady* was set in the Regency period. 'I jot down ideas from anywhere,' she told me. 'Driving along sometimes, I have to stop, whip out my notepad and scribble sentences, names, anything that comes. I sometimes think I get my best ideas when I'm washing up, which makes for very soggy notes I promise you, but is worth it.'

She starts work every day between 9 and 9.30 a.m. in her study, writes without a break until 2 p.m. when she will have lunch and perhaps take a walk – 'Exercise is very important for a writer, who is, let's face it, sitting down for a great proportion of her time' – and she will often go back to work in the evening if a book is going well. 'I'm very anti-social when I'm writing, and tend to shut myself completely off from the world. My children were sent swimming so often one summer when I was thus engaged that they complained their skin was becoming prune-like!'

She added, 'I think onto the typewriter, which is fortunate because my handwriting is so abysmal I wouldn't be able to read it back. I recently bought a word processor, which has speeded up my writing considerably. I prefer historical romances to modern, and I sincerely hope I will always be what I am now – a compulsive writer.'

Margery Hilton was one of the writers whose books I had particularly enjoyed during my market research, and when I had my first Mills & Boon accepted, she wrote welcoming me to the club, and we have kept in touch ever since. She had her first book accepted in 1966 and has now written twenty-six.

She told me that she began writing more by accident than design after a back injury had forced her to give up her theatrical interests (she was a professional dancer before she met and married the stage manager, and had always been involved with, and loved, the theatre). 'I had always scribbled short stories and bits and pieces, but never with a thought of publication,' she told me. 'But during my last year in the theatre I was greatly encouraged by a theatrical colleague who read pieces I had written and urged me to write more, and this triggered off the desire to write and finish a novel. I began one, then put it away for a while as I was involved in so many other activities – running a children's dance school, teaching movement and dance therapy at a hospital for mentally handicapped children, for instance. But after the injury I was tied to the house for a while and to save myself from going mad, I wrote a book, sent it off to Mills & Boon and had it accepted within three weeks!'

I asked her if she had any particular method of working. 'Several,' she answered, 'at first, anyway. I'd often write a piece that appealed to me, and it would go in the middle of the book. Probably something to do with my theatrical training, where items are rehearsed in no particular sequence. Then I decided to try and write thinking directly onto a typewriter. Because I wasn't sure at first if this would work, I started typing a rough draft of a book onto some ancient pink paper I had picked up cheaply from a sale. By the time it was half-way through it was flowing so well I didn't dare go back and begin again or I'd lose the thread so I kept on. And Alan Boon phoned, asked me if I'd anything for them and I told him what was happening. 'Finish it as it is,' he said. Which probably makes me the first writer who has sent in a typescript on passionate pink paper!'

'Where do you get your ideas?' was my next, inevitable question.

'I don't know,' she answered. 'From music – I find the classics, also romantic singers, are a good source of inspiration. But as for my heroes and heroines, I can only think they come from somewhere in my subconscious. Can I tell you something very interesting that happened once half-way through a book?'

I assured her I was all ears. 'I was writing a book, and one evening I stopped, went into what I can only describe as a sort of dream state, and "heard" the sea in my mind, and saw a green shadowy grove. That image, and the sound of the sea haunted me for six weeks, whilst I was finishing my novel. Then again one evening I went into a daydream and "saw" the grove again, this time with a child standing there. That picture stayed with me for several days. Then I saw a young woman in the grove as well … finally, days later, I saw a man, very clearly. I knew the woman was a dancer, I knew the man was a widower and I knew that, somehow, the child would be the crux of the book. I had no choice but to write it, and it was called *The Whispering Grove*.' Now I know why that book of hers is one of my favourites!

To summarise briefly: What all these women have in common is that they are compulsive writers, and disciplined in their approach to work. Overheard snatches of conversation, a word, a line in a magazine or newspaper, a picture, a place, an image, a house – all have played their part in inspiring them. Although their methods of putting these glorious images on to paper may differ, the end result is the same. A book!

'Why doesn't somebody interview you for your book?' Eileen Jackson asked me.

'Because I'm writing it,' I answered.

'So?' she said. Which leads me on to my next interview, with a writer of whom you may not have heard, a modest person called

Mary Wibberley. I met her in front of a mirror.

'How long have you been writing?' I asked her. 'All my life,' she told me, 'ever since I first picked up a pencil. And even before I could read books, I was reading them, if you see what I mean.'

'No,' I told her. 'I don't see.'

'Well, I'd pick them up, open them, study the little squiggly black marks and pretend I could read, making up all sorts of nonsense, which impressed my other two-year-old friends immensely because they couldn't read either.'

'Oh, I see.' I went on, 'Where do you get your ideas from?'

'Everyone asks me this,' she replied. 'And the answer is I don't *know*, any more than you do. Ideas come from everywhere. It's as though a writer plucks them from the air. A thought, an image, a snatch of music heard distantly – anything can trigger off a sentence which can grow into a book. It's lovely.'

'Are you disciplined in your writing?' I asked her.

'Yes,' she said. 'Next question.'

'Do you consider yourself a normal human being?'

'Is anybody?' she sighed. 'Especially a writer. I mean, we see the world differently, don't we? And in any case, if I were normal, I wouldn't be standing here talking to myself in a mirror, would I?'

I had to agree with that. 'One last question,' I said. (I could see she was impatient to leave, probably to get back to writing.) 'Is there any book you could recommend for aspiring romantic novelists?'

'Mmm, well,' she said after a moment's thought. 'There is one called *To Writers with Love*, but I can't remember who it's by, and anyway, I've got better things to do than stand talking to you all day – goodbye.' And with that she left. Really! Some people …

TEN

Beyond The Bedroom Door

GO into any bookshop and look around for a few minutes; you will realise that there are some extremely explicit modern romances being published. I mean, of course, sexually explicit. I've read some contemporary romances the explicitness of which would make your hair curl! The dictionary definition of romance is as follows: 'Any fictitious or wonderful tale, *a romantic occurrence or series of same. A love affair; romantic atmosphere or feeling.*' And now the word explicit. Ready? '*Not implied but distinctly stated*: plain in language: outspoken: clear: unreserved.'

The italics are mine, and those of the first definition do not link up with those of the second. Most readers of romantic novels do not want to read in clinical detail an explicit description of everything that the hero, in his love-making, does to the heroine, and vice-versa. But they do want to know what she experiences when he looks at her or touches her, and they do want to be able to use their imagination. If everything is spelt out with anatomical precision they don't get the chance. If a would-be romantic scene reads like a sex manual it is not romantic. Some modern romances are merely a succession of sexual encounters between hero and heroine with very little plot and even less romance. Readers eventually become bored with this, and turn to the romantic novels in which they can identify with the heroine all the way through. It is important for a new writer to establish in her mind before she embarks on any love scenes exactly what she wishes to convey to the reader. Sexual tension is built up gradually by the skilful writer, subtly conveyed by a look, a

touch, a vivid awareness between the hero and heroine that affects
the other characters in the book. Have you ever been in a crowd of
people at a party, talking to a woman friend, and been made
suddenly aware that her lover has walked in? I have. She neither
looked directly at him nor acknowledged his presence, but she
changed in an instant. I could almost feel the vibrations from
where I stood, and looked casually towards the doorway to see his
eyes hungrily upon her, aware of no one else in that room. It was
as though a current of electricity passed between them. They
vanished shortly afterwards, to no one's surprise, certainly not
mine. The atmosphere between them sizzled, there is no other way
to describe it. If you can convey that on paper, you'll have a
winner. Did I make notes? You bet I did, as soon as I could escape
to the bathroom. Loo paper is not the best for writing on, but
when it's all there is, it suffices.

If the question – will they or won't they? – is answered on page
three with hero and heroine hopping into bed for the first time,
and at frequent intervals afterwards, then there is no way you can
build up sexual tension in a romantic novel. The only question will
be how many times they'll manage to make love before the end of
the book. If that's what you want to write, go ahead, but you
won't expect your reader to go through the book in trembling
anticipation for the joys in store, will you? If she's been tasting that
delicious forbidden fruit from page three onwards she might well
have a jaded palate by page two hundred!

To ignore totally the part that sex plays in a romantic novel
would be naïve. Romantic love naturally involves sex sooner or
later – preferably later – but in a romantic novel bed-hopping at
the beginning is a turn-off. The actress Jacqueline Bisset was
interviewed in a newspaper last year, and talking about sex in
films, said, 'Desire and pursuit are much more interesting than the
act itself. Do it in the third reel and the rest of the movie is very
anticlimactic.' She had summed it up beautifully, and what she said
is equally appropriate to books. The key factor in blending sex and
romance is that magic quality vital to all fiction – imagination. We
the writers must be subtle enough to allow the reader to give full
rein to her imaginative powers.

There was one occasion I still remember vividly when this
worked rather too well. It was in 1973, and a dedicated reader of

Mills & Boon at that time was a Dutch woman who wrote to them frequently to say which books she enjoyed. I was having lunch with Alan Boon and Frances Whitehead, my editor, when he told me that the woman had written in to tell them how much she had enjoyed my fifth book *The Man at La Valaise*. Believe me, there is no greater boost to a writer's ego than that! However, I managed a modest smile, as he went on, in rather puzzled tones: 'She said she thought the rape scene was very well handled.' I nearly fell off my chair! Equally puzzled and horrified I managed to squeak, 'But he didn't rape her, honestly.' I had visions of being asked to leave at once and never darken their door again. In 1973, hero and heroine did not go to bed together, still less was there rape. I came home and read the book through not once, but twice. Could I have written a rape scene without even knowing it? No, I knew I hadn't, but there was one scene where the heroine, Sacha is forced to share a bedroom in a remote Provençal cottage with her kidnapper Nicolai Torlenkov, and she tries to escape, and ends up briefly on a bed with him and, well, I *suppose*, if that reader's imagination had been in overdrive when she had read that part she could have misinterpreted what was *almost* totally innocent. The point is that no one else thought so – or at least no one wrote in to complain! One old lady I knew told me that she had enjoyed the book as well. She had liked the touch of mystery in it. But she never mentioned rape at all. Perhaps the moral of that is: it's not so much what you write, as what you make your readers see.

Up until about twelve years ago, the heroes and heroines of contemporary romances never went to bed together. More recently, say five or six years ago, they did, very occasionally, make love before they were married, but it had to be made quite clear that they were deeply in love and intending to wed, and the love-making happened 'off-stage' as it were. The scope has broadened considerably since then, and nowadays, almost anything goes, which in my opinion is a pity, for when the limits of descriptive licence are reached, what on earth can happen next? The mind boggles.

If there is anyone reading this book who wants to learn how to write vividly explicit love-making scenes, there are plenty of books on the market prepared to tell them how. This is not one of them. Men and women who are unmarried and romantically involved do go to bed together, and they do make love, I'm sure we're all agreed on that, and as it happens in real life, so it happens in novels. But is it necessary to describe in lurid detail what is essentially a very private act? Some writers think so. Many do not.

There is a marvellous scene in the film of *Gone With The Wind*, where Rhett Butler, seething with passion and frustration, storms up the stairs, carrying Scarlett O'Hara. The scene immediately after that shows Scarlett, a very satisfied woman indeed, sitting up in bed, preening herself and looking rather smug. The audience is left in no doubt about what happened in the interim. If you can convey such powerful sexual imagery on paper, you will have a very sensuous book.

Both *Jane Eyre* and *Wuthering Heights* crackle with sexual tension all the way through, yet neither could be said to be explicit in any way. In the film *The Thomas Crown Affair* the scene where Faye Dunaway and Steve McQueen play chess will be remembered long after the rest of the film is forgotten, simply because of the sizzling undercurrents of sexual awareness – and the sure knowledge of what was to follow.

In sharp contrast are the memoirs of films stars that are so often published in Sunday papers where lip-smacking details are given of their affairs with other film stars. Go on, admit it, you've read them too. But could you remember them a day later? I couldn't, and I'll bet you couldn't either.

The secret of writing successful romance lies in keeping your reader in breathless anticipation of the joys to come – and to allow her to use her imagination when those scenes happen. On a more practical level, it is far easier to write passionate prose late at night, when everyone has gone to bed and you are alone, than it is on a cold rainy Monday morning! Picture the scene. It is nearly midnight, the house is quiet save for your favourite mood music playing softly in the background. There are no telephones about to ring, no one likely to call at the door, just you, and your hero and heroine waiting in the wings, as it were, for the action to begin. You don't know what is going to happen any more than they do, but if they are in a romantic place, and the mood is right, who knows? This is the joy of writing, the venturing into the unknown. Just relax and go along with them. You know them both well, they are living, breathing human beings; they may surprise *you*.

The reader of a romantic novel wants to get involved with the characters, to identify with the heroine and to live in the book while she is reading it. For her to be able to do this, you must have done all these things first. So don't write anything that makes you feel uncomfortable, because she will be aware of that fact. There is a wide range of types of romantic novel even within the same series from the same publisher, and all have their faithful readers. The choice is up to you. You can only ever write what you would enjoy reading, remember that.

ELEVEN

A Rose By Any Other Name

VANESSA is dark-haired, tall and strikingly attractive. Renata is statuesque, blazingly honest and with a strong personality, while Sally is a red-head with temper to match her hair. And Jan, of course, is rebellious and spirited. How do I know? These are the heroines' names as I saw and used them in four of my novels. Names *do* help to conjure up pictures and personalities of their owners.

Janna was an orphaned waif, living in precarious circumstances in a South American shanty town, who was rescued from terrible trouble by the hero and brought back to England. I could not have called her anything else but *I don't know why*.

You may see Genevieve as small, blonde and humorous, but I don't. To me she has auburn hair, green eyes, and is tall and slender. My Genevieve would therefore be a vastly different character from yours, but that doesn't matter, because yours will behave consistently with the personality you know is right for her, just as mine will. What is important is that you choose a name you feel happy with, one which fits your heroine like a glove. Carry that chosen name around with you for a few days before you begin writing about her. Taste it, say it out loud (not in a crowded supermarket: you may be disappointed by whoever looks round in answer and that could put you off!); 'see' her moving about in your mind's eye and you will know if you have chosen well.

I started a book once and was half-way through Chapter One when I realised that something was making me unhappy about it.

I had given my heroine the wrong name. I went back to the beginning, crossed out all references to it, had a good solid think, and then knew where I had gone wrong. The book was *With This Ring*. I had called the heroine Sara. I changed it to Siana, and that was it! Sara was right as the heroine in *Man of Power*, but not in that other book. Don't ask me why because I don't know. We writers can be illogical at the best of times, and that's part of the fun.

There is an American actor in the TV series *Hill Street Blues*, with the most glorious name, Taurean Blacque. And there was once an ice skating star called Ty Babalonia. Aren't those superb? Jayne Torvill's name is equally attractive, as is Marisa Berenson's. In fact, a lot of well-known people have extremely interesting names. I've never understood why Lucille le Sueur and Spangler Arlington Brugh were persuaded to change theirs. Think how those would have looked in lights outside cinemas! They achieved fame anyway as Joan Crawford and Robert Taylor. They might have got there quicker though.

There are so many sources of delicious names, first and probably most obvious is a book of baby's names, obtainable from any good bookshop. Meanings are given as well, which can link up nicely with your characters.

Another rich source is television. I watch the credits at the end of films and plays with as much interest as the films themselves. Sometimes more! Keep your pen and paper handy, though, or you will have forgotten them five minutes later. This is where it helps to have a video. Some of the American films have anything up to fifty names, at least half of them quite exotic and certainly unusual. If you don't believe me, try this for size. I played back the ending of the film *Mr Billion*, starring Terence Hill (a very dishy hero, by the way) and copied the following down: Nate Long, Sheldon Schrager, Peter Bogart, Arne Schmidt, Marshall Schlom, Robert Barrere, Clifford C. Kohlweck, Alain Chammas, Leo Lolito (!) Jack Lannorelli, Rick Martens, Victor Tourjansky, Joe Chavalier, Darren Knight, Earl Boen, Dan Lee Gant, Denver Mattson, Henry Kinji, Clay Brayden, Bill Jobe, Mel Pape, Seth Bank. There were more ... Try juggling them around.

Notice how many heroes have Christian names beginning with the 'hard' letters, such as B, G, J, K, R, V. Hard names for hard men? Of course. If you have no books on names, your television's on the blink, and you need a name immediately, then go for that good old standby, the telephone directory. Or you may just get inspiration from the list below, of a few of the names I've used for my heroes with their meanings.

Blaise: *torch*

Boris: *battler*

Brand: *firebrand*

Brent: *steep hill*

Bryce: *swift*

Gareth: *firm spear*

Gavin: *hawk*

Grant: *great one*

Gregor: *watchful one*

Kyle: *from the Scottish strait*

Lachlan: *warlike*

Luke: *light*

Morgan: *sea dweller*

Roarke: *famous ruler*

Ryan: *little king*

Vargen: *meaning not known — I think I made this one up!*

Now for heroines:

Alisa: *truth*

Andrea: *womanly*

Beth: *oath of God*

Catriona: *pure one*

Charlotte: *womanly one*

Elena: *light*

Gemma: *a gem*

Helen: *light*

Joanna: *Grace of the Lord*

Polly: *diminutive of Mary, Star of the Sea*

Sally: *Princess*

Tara: *rocky pinnacle*

Vanessa: *a butterfly*

Victoria: *victory*

There are literally hundreds more of course, in any name book, and it's fascinating to look up the meanings.

Surnames are of equal importance, especially for the hero. The heroine will be changing her name to his when they marry so make sure, by saying them out loud, that they sound right. I forgot this golden rule when writing *The Taming of Tamsin*. The hero's name? Blaise Torran. Hers? Tamsin, Tammy for short. It wasn't until right at the end that I realised, so I made a joke of it on the very last lines, as follows: ' "And I love you, Blaise Torran. Oh, no – Tammy Torran, can you imagine?" Laughing, they set off to drive back to the cottage to tell the others – as if they needed telling.' No, not to tell them about the name, but that they were getting married – oh, never mind!

Anyway, back to surnames for your heroes. Again, hard names are a must. Need I add that a hero called Albert Coward might not go down so well with the readers as one called Dominic Steele? Albert may well be a charming man, but his name lacks that essential macho ring to it. The baby book of names can be useful, for a lot of Christian names can also be used as surnames — for example, Garrett, Grant, Craig, Saber, Bramwell, Varian, Garrick, and so on. The search can be fun, and a sufficiently interesting name can help to provide you with a title for your book. *That Man Bryce, The Benedict Man, Logan's Island, Kyle's Kingdom*: I've used those and more because they appealed very much.

TWELVE

Meet Your Publisher, Meet Your Public

WHAT is a publisher? Let's begin by saying what a publisher is not. He is not a philanthropist who is in business to put into print your works of art whether or not they have any chance of selling. He is not a man who publishes only the works of his sons, daughters, nephews, maiden aunts and other assorted relatives. And he is not a man who sits in an ivory tower remote from the realities of everyday life.

A publisher is a businessman. In the same way that some men sell houses, holidays or cars, he sells books. He depends on what he sells for his living, and if he doesn't sell those books he is jeopardising that livelihood, and the chances of his other books. So he selects what he publishes with care. He is also something of a gambler as he is expected to take a risk on outsiders – new writers, complete unknowns, offering manuscripts which may fall outside his normal range but might, just might, prove to be winners. He cannot say with certainty in advance what will be a world-wide best-seller although he may have certain sneaking suspicions.

The publisher employs a variety of specialists, but those who will most concern you at the initial stages are his readers and his editors. When you submit your manuscript to a publishing house it will first pass through the hands of one or more readers who are employed to sort the wheat from the chaff. They will read through your work and give a frank report on it (which you will never see!); from long experience, these readers know precisely what the publisher wants in terms of length, content, style, and treatment, and they will make their recommendations accordingly. They will not recommend on the strength of your name, your family relationship with said publisher, the colour of typing paper you use, or the pretty ribbons you wrapped it with. Their sole concern is the suitability of your work for their lists. If your precious first-born survives this scrutiny it will be handed to an editor, who will also read it with a keen, perceptive eye, and if she thinks, hey, this is just what we want, she will pass it on to the man himself. (Here I must apologise. I am referring to the publisher as 'he' when there are of course, several women publishers, as there are male editors. It just makes for easier reading instead of writing he/she all the time.)

If he decides to publish, you will receive a letter of acceptance, followed shortly afterwards by a contract setting out details of payment. Never sign a contract that gives a publisher all rights in your book. The book is your property, the copyright is yours, and should remain so. (The publisher – or literary agent – is, however, nearly always better equipped to sell rights such as American, translation, paperback, television, etc., and these may therefore be left in his hands – but the author generally receives the major share of the monies received.) If you feel uneasy about any contract, contact the Society of Authors, who are very helpful, and are always looking after the interests of writers (once you have had a book accepted you will be eligible for membership, anyway). As for payment, reputable publishers usually offer an advance against royalties. Once the advance is earned back through sales of the book, the author starts receiving royalty payments, yearly or twice a year; these are based on a small percentage (generally between $7\frac{1}{2}$ and 15 per cent of the selling price of every copy sold, or, for sales abroad, a percentage of the publisher's receipts.)

So far, I have been talking about what I think of as 'proper' publishers, but there is another kind – the so-called 'vanity' publishers – that I do not recommend. You pay them to publish your book, and publish it they will. But you will be the loser, for, in spite of all their assurances, they are unlikely to make any effort to promote, market or sell your book. After all, they have nothing to lose if they don't sell a single copy – you've already paid them. Proper publishers – however disappointed an author may be with the sales of his or her masterpiece – do try to promote and sell their books, for they have taken the risk and spent their own money. If you are really desperate to see your work in print, and cannot find a publisher to take it on, then publish it yourself – that, too, has its problems, as you will find out – but do not be seduced by those advertisements that invite writers to send in their manuscripts for publication (real publishers don't advertise like this). And do remember that if a book is worth publishing, it will eventually find a publisher.

You may decide that, rather than approach a publisher direct, you would prefer to have a literary agent. I don't have one, but many of my writer friends do. In very simple terms an agent is someone who will read and assess your manuscript in hopes of finding it a saleable work, and will take a percentage of your royalties (usually ten to fifteen per cent for sales in Great Britain, and fifteen per cent for foreign markets) when he sells the work. The choice is a personal one. I am happier dealing directly with Frances Whitehead, my editor at Mills & Boon, with whom I get on very well, and I have no need for an agent.

But whether you decide to send your book to an agent or directly to a publisher, there are certain basic rules of professionalism to observe. I mention some in Chapter 13, 'Purely Practical', but a little repetition won't hurt. Don't submit a tatty, dog-eared typescript to anyone. Present a clean, clearly typed book, double-spaced, on A4-size paper, with every page numbered, and with your name (and pseudonym if any) and address typed on the covering sheet, as well as in your brief letter. It is not only professional, it is good manners to do so. Oh, and by the way, don't forget the stamped addressed envelope. That's the end of the little lecture on manners. But it is the beginning of something else when publication day arrives ...

'Who will buy my book?' I hear you cry. Library purchases guarantee a certain number of sales, but what you really mean by that question is, I suspect, 'Who are the readers of romantic novels?' You may be pleasantly surprised by the answer, which I was given by Peter H. Mann, until recently head of Sociology at Sheffield University. Since the late sixties, Dr Mann has carried out readership surveys for Mills & Boon on this very subject. The first completed survey in 1969 came from 2,500 replies to questionnaires sent out by him. The results, along with those of another done in 1973 were carefully analysed by Dr Mann with the eye of a trained scientific observer with no particular axe to grind for Mills & Boon.

I spoke to Dr Mann recently and put to him that most obvious of all questions: 'Who reads romantic novels?' His reply was fascinating, and dispelled some hoary old myths right at the start. ' "They" say that romantic novels are read by housewives stuck at home with two or more young children and nothing better to do. "They" say romantic novels are read by women who never read anything else. "They" say only women of limited education read them. *All wrong.*'

I don't know who the ubiquitous 'they' are any more than you, but don't they have a lot of opinions? Back to Dr Mann. He went on: 'The readership of Mills & Boon, and of all types of romantic novels covers a broad spectrum. Ten per cent of the reading public of romantic novels embraces such professions as women doctors, lawyers, dentists, and so on.'

Surprised? Don't be. He then went on to tell me that thirty per cent of the women who are reading a book at this moment are reading romantic fiction. So that means that we, the writers, are catering for the most popular genre. Dr Mann admitted that when he first began his research he himself nursed some of the assumptions about romantic fiction which he was to encounter in others.

His work revealed that readers of romantic fiction come not only from a wide range of age groups but also from the whole spectrum of social classes, occupations and marital states. The theory of the frustrated spinster went out of the window when it was revealed that a large percentage of readers were not only married but often young married women with a modern outlook on love and marriage. He found that readers lived in every area of Great Britain and, more recently of course, in many other countries. One interesting feature in recent years has been the expansion in readership beyond the United Kingdom and the Commonwealth into many countries in the Middle and Far East, and South America. Every now and then the postman comes with a large parcel for me from Mills & Boon. Over the last few years I have received literally dozens of foreign language editions of my books, as diverse as Japanese, Greek, Afrikaans, Portuguese (for Brazil), Finnish, Swedish, Italian, French, Serbo-Croat, Dutch, and Turkish. I didn't realise I could write in all these languages! I was present at the launch party for Mills & Boon's entry into Holland in 1975 under the Dutch-language imprint 'Bouquet Reeks'. I met several of the translators and saw the Dutch television commercials due to be launched to promote the series. The champagne flowed freely – it was a *wonderful* party!

Speaking of languages, I was intrigued to learn from Dr Mann that the Oxford University Press, in their 'Alpha Books' series, have adapted a number of romantic novels (including several of mine) as reading text for foreign students learning English. This fact must counter the accusations made by certain literary people that romantic novels are poorly written.

Let's remember, however, that readerships change as time goes on. The typical reader of the forties and fifties is different in every way from her sister in these eighties. Basically they all want the same thing – a good romantic story, well constructed and well written. Today's women are likely to hold a much wider range of jobs, take more exotic holidays, and have more modern attitudes to everything from women's liberation to sexual relationships. You, the romantic novelist of today, must expect to do much of your own research. Read the latest novels, eavesdrop shamelessly in W.H. Smith's, notice trends in women's magazines and generally make sure that your characters are with it. Popularity lists are often published in newspapers and magazines showing sales figures for all books. You can see exactly what people are reading.

In the last five years there has been a tremendous upsurge of media interest in romantic novels. You will be as aware as I am of the number of newspaper and magazine articles, radio features and television programmes on this subject. I've lost count of the cuttings I've taken, and the programmes I've seen, in this last year alone. I've taken part in five television programmes in the last five years, and had more than a dozen radio interviews. All great fun; I told you I was a ham at heart. While these programmes and articles have varied in their attitudes to romantic fiction, it is still encouraging to know that notice is now being taken of this kind of writing – it's as though media people may love 'em or hate 'em, but feel they can no longer ignore 'em! I feel this growth of interest can only augur well for our kind of writing. People's attitudes will not change overnight, but at least we're being *noticed*!

Dr Mann told me to ask this question of every would-be romantic best-selling author: 'Have you got fifty books inside you? The most successful romantic novelists write prolifically and sustain that writing over a period of years.' If you have one beautiful book inside you, fine, go ahead and write it, but don't expect to become a best-seller, will you? He continued: 'If you can write three or four books a year that's a different story altogether. The most popular writers are those who do that, and more, and have their own following among readers.'

We are in the business of selling, and if you can write the books the readers want to read, you will sell. Romantic novels are escapism. You want to write about realism? Life with a capital L, warts and all, gritty down-to-earth novels which will shatter your readers' complacency? Fine. Go ahead. But you will be writing for a different market from the one we are talking about in this book.

THIRTEEN

Purely Practical

I'VE said that all a writer needs is pen, paper, and a fertile imagination, and that is true, as far as the actual writing goes. But when your potential best-selling romantic novel is written, and you decide to send it off to a publisher, ah, then, the rude world intrudes.

Publishers do not accept handwritten manuscripts. What they want is a typescript. Neat, double-spaced with wide margins and preferably on A4-size paper. So that is what you will give them, keeping at least one carbon for yourself. There are several choices open to you here. You can type it yourself, you can persuade a friend to type it for you, you can take it to one of the many typing agencies, you can do it on a word processor or you can advertise in your local paper for a home typist. Whatever is best for you is the ideal choice. Let's take the first one: typing the manuscript yourself. This has several advantages, one of which is that the precious book will be in your possession so there's no chance of it getting lost/stolen/or having a bottle of ink spilt on it – the greatest advantage of all is that, as you sit down to copy it onto the machine from your handwriting, you will undoubtedly see minor faults and alterations that you can then put right. But you might not be able to type, or possess a typewriter. Do not worry! It's easy to learn typing, and if you can't afford a machine you can hire one for a week or two – I advise hiring an electric model. Believe me, I've used both in my time, before I could afford a typist and electric is better (but try and keep a manual handy in case of power cuts!)

I typed my first manuscript on a Corona portable, a second-hand one I had bought for £12 (a lot of money twenty years ago). Then, when my first book was accepted, my dear husband bought me an Adler electric. (I instantly took back all I had ever said about him being a male chauvinist pig, of course!). I still, occasionally, type a book myself, if I know I want to make alterations as I go along. But generally I hire ex-secretary friends to type for me, which has two pluses. One is that they earn some money (and I pay above the going rate); the second is that they can phone me if there's a word they can't read (yes, that does sometimes happen) and I can tell them in moments without holding up the work.

Taking your manuscript to a typing agency can be fairly expensive, but you will get a presentable typescript, so if you can afford it, go ahead.

Word processors. Ah, yes. A great many writers have them nowadays, and the advantages here are of course, *perfect* typescripts, for you can erase any errors before printing out. The 'ah, yes' was because I am the most unmechanically minded woman you'll ever meet. It took me a week to master the remote control on our video. It took me even longer to learn how to play Space Invaders on my son's computer game. I do not understand computers, I do not wish to understand computers. One day I may desire to learn, when they can be programmed to take over a kitchen and provide three-course meals for hungry families but until then I shall say pass.

But for you who know instantly what floppy discs and bytes are (lucky you), they're fine. Several of my friends have them and rave about them, and when I receive letters from them, they are a joy to behold, immaculate, quite beautiful.

If you advertise in your local paper for a home typist, and he or she possesses one of those wonderous machines, you are truly fortunate.

Practical matters part two coming up. Reference books. That is, the very basic ones to make your writing life that bit easier — and even more fun. The basics are these: a good dictionary; a book of synonyms; a book of quotations; *The Writers' and Artists' Yearbook*. There are more of course. There are probably *thousands* more, and you might have them all, but they won't make you a good writer, only you can do that.

The good dictionary hardly needs explanation, does it? Mine is the Chambers 20th Century, it cost me £10.95, and it has all the words I'll ever need.

My book of synonyms is the best I have ever seen – I've had several small ones over the years, but I discovered this a year ago in a bookshop, bought it, brought it home. A writer friend who visited me a few days later from a remote area of Scotland clapped her eyes on it, shrieked, 'I *must* have this, and I can't get one where I live,' so I sold it to her and had to go and buy myself another one (moral: don't show your writer friends your reference books unless you have shares in the publishing company). It's *The Synonym Finder*, published by Rodale, price a little wince-making at £14, but worth it. For instance, it has sixty-one definitions of the word 'virile' – which is what all our heroes are, of course, and now you have sixty-one ways of telling your reader so. And for 'spirited' (as all best heroines should be) you get sixty-six ways to express it. Do you know, counting through these has given me ideas for another romantic novel.

A book of quotations is another essential. One for the sheer beauty of some of the quotes, another for titles. Remember *Ill Met By Moonlight* (from Shakespeare's *A Midsummer Night's Dream*), *Fair Stood the Wind for France* (from Michael Drayton, 'Ballad of Agincourt'); Hemingway's *For Whom the Bell Tolls* is from John Donne, and *The Sun also Rises* from the Bible. That list is almost endless. I have three books of quotations but the longest of them, and therefore most comprehensive, is Bartlett's. There should be a warning printed on every book of quotations. It is fatal to try and look up anything when you have only a little time – unless, unlike me, you are capable of searching for what you want without being sidetracked by the thousands of delicious snippets that proliferate. ('Enter these enchanted woods you who dare': George Meredith. See what I mean?)

The Writers' and Artists' Yearbook has so many practical applications that it is an essential. First, for its list of publishers, secondly for its articles about publishing, and income tax, and its list of writers' agents; equally important are its pages of proof correction signs for *when* your first novel is accepted. You will need that list, believe me. I still keep mine by me when I'm proof correcting. The one I can never get right is for the deletion of a letter. I can never remember it and if I were asked to describe it I would have to say that it's a little squiggle somewhat like a demented tadpole. But I need to *see* it every time and if I didn't have my *Writers' and Artists' Yearbook*, I wouldn't be able to.

Lastly, among the miscellania of a writer's life, you will need the following – not necessarily in this order:

Several envelope-type folders – about twenty pence from any stationer's – for keeping manuscripts clean and in some sort of order. Large envelopes, stamps (plenty!), writing paper (for your letter to the editor; more of that below), Sellotape, pens, pencils, 'white ink' for erasing mistakes on manuscript or typescripts, oh yes, and paper. Stapler, paper clips, elastic bands. Don't ask me what those last three are for. I only know that when I need them I can never find any, so be more organised than me, keep them in a box. Did you know that the majority of writers are extremely disorganised and lead lives of total chaos? You didn't? Just to let you know you are not alone. That makes you feel better, I know. I've never yet visited any writer friends and found their studies immaculate. (I would be suspicious if I did.) Mine is a joyful mess, the despair of my cleaner, but I know where everything is, well, *most* of it – well, some of it most of the time and I do try, honest – but enough. Now to the letter you're going to send to the editor of the publishers you have decided to favour with your masterpiece. This is important. *Make it brief*. I have seen, and heard of, twelve-page missives to editors from would-be writers, detailing their life story, their reasons for writing the book, their financial situation which makes it imperative the book be accepted, the names and ages of their children (and possibly their nieces and nephews only I never got that far and neither did the editors).

I'm going to give you an example of the sort of letter that editors appreciate. Don't feel you have to copy it word for word, but study it and then write something of similar brevity. First, try and find out the name of the editor at your chosen publishers. They really do appreciate a personally addressed letter rather than Dear Sir/Madam. And it might possibly get to him/her much more quickly, which is what you want. So here goes.

'Wits End'
4 The Willows,
East Twittering,
Cheshire CH99 1LU
30th June 1985

Miss P. Brown,
Messrs Gallop & Tweed Ltd,
18–22 Writer's Way,
London W1

Dear Miss Brown,

I am enclosing my romantic novel *A Kiss Before Dawn* for your consideration. It is approximately 55,000 words in length. I also enclose return postage.

Yours sincerely,

Amelia Bloggs

AMELIA BLOGGS (MISS)

(Even if your signature is legible, type your name underneath it.)

That's all. Couldn't be simpler, could it? To the typescript you affix a stamped, self-addressed envelope large enough to take it. No, not being pessimistic, just good-mannered – and that goes down well too. She doesn't need, or want, your life story. All she wants is your clean, perfectly typed book. That is her job, to find new writers, and believe me, she will be delighted if she can say yes. You should receive an acknowledgement of receipt after, say, a week, and by that time you will be already well into your next book, won't you? If you're not, you haven't been paying attention to this one.

Next comes an item that really ought to have gone in near the beginning, with the reference books, because it is as important. The fact that it didn't proves that I'm not as organised as I think I am which should give new hope to everyone. The item is this: COLLECTING. And for your collection you will need folders or large envelopes. And these folders should be neatly labelled with the following headings: Locations. Houses. Heroes.

Heroines. Careers. Food. Furniture. Flora and Fauna. And you may be able to think of several more which I haven't thought of, but these are some of the most useful categories.

All writers have their collections, and in them are newspaper and magazine cuttings garnered over a period of time, and they are very precious, believe me. If you haven't yet started yours, I'll tell you how to begin.

LOCATIONS

The brochures from travel agents have marvellous pictures, so does the *National Geographical Magazine*, issues of which you will often be able to buy for a few pence from second-hand bookstalls. I recently bought a dozen (I couldn't manage to carry more) for fifteen pence each and they have superb photographs in them, and are perhaps better left intact on your bookshelves because the articles are equally good source material. If you go abroad, take as many pictures of backgrounds as you can afford. If you don't go abroad, persuade your friends who do to send you postcards – or, better still, bring lots back with them because postcards are treated as 5th-class mail by most foreign countries and rarely arrive. You will soon have built up a rich and colourful library of settings for your books at no great cost.

HOUSES

Houses are my special weakness I must now confess, and the best sources of all are *Country Life* and estate agents' catalogues. When I was writing *Man of Power*, I used six photographs from an advertisement in *Country Life* of a villa in the South of France (*extremely* pricey, need I add!) for the hero, Morgan Haldane's home. The photographs were of the interior as well as the exterior, and there was a superb swimming pool. By the time I had finished the book, I felt as though I had been there and lived in that villa. A year ago on holiday in Aberdeen, we were taken to Meldrum House, a country hotel in Old Meldrum, and I fell in love with it even as we went up the drive, took lots of photographs, came home a week later, started writing a book set there, and had my hero and heroine snowbound for a week (alone). I reversed the syllables, called it Drummell House; the book, *Linked from the Past*, came out recently. This year we returned there and I told the manager that his hotel had inspired me to write a book, so he let me wander around and take more photographs. One, in a bedroom, with me sitting on a superb four-poster bed, has given me several more ideas ...

HEROES

Men. Attractive men. Lots and lots of photographs of these, ready to be taken out and studied at leisure when a book is in the pre-planning stage, the 'what if ...' stage, when ideas are amorphous, and no picture has yet emerged. Film stars are an obvious choice. Richard Gere is very dishy, so were Rock Hudson and James Garner when younger, but there will be an occasional male model advertising clothes whose looks appeal to you. Cut the photograph out, add it to your collection, and one day you will be glad you did because he'll be the right one for your next book. All kinds of magazines are your source for these. The Sunday colour supplements are rich in advertising material. Just keep a pair of scissors handy at all times.

HEROINES

Same sources as for heroes. I find the make-up ads a bit boring. The women tend to have rather wooden expressions, and those modelling clothes, particularly in *Cosmopolitan* and other glossy monthlies, seem to prefer to pout or scowl at the camera, but there's still a wide choice. Snip away.

CAREERS

For both main characters, articles on successful businessmen and women can provide a rich store of information. I recently cut one out of our local paper about the first woman to work on an oil rig (she's a radio operator). I've not yet decided to set one on an oil rig, but if I do, I have a good start. Helicopter pilot, company director, head of firm catering for dinner parties in the houses of the wealthy, magazine editor, deep-sea diver, antique repairer, photographer, artist, restaurant owner, television producer – I have cuttings about all these and more, and either your hero *or* heroine could be any of these things, and if you're still stuck, let your fingers do the walking through the index at the back of Yellow Pages and if you decide it might be ideal for your heroine to be running a boarding kennels, pick up the telephone and ask if you can go and look round – and take your camera with you.

FOOD

No, you don't have to give detailed descriptions of everything your hero and heroine eat as they sit looking at each other over a candle-lit dinner, but it helps you to convey the picture more vividly if you *know*. Again, the magazine recipe pages will provide beautiful colour pictures for you to drool over. (It needs extra will-power if you're trying to diet but it's all in the cause of your art.) And if you bring home menus from wherever you've been eating out you can have your heroine dismissing the ratatouille quite knowledgeably – *and* be able to spell it without searching through the dictionary, provided that the restaurant owner can spell!

FURNITURE

Antique and modern. Pictures of modern furniture are in most magazines, but for antique furniture again *Country Life* is an excellent source of photographs, *Millers Guide* is also full of them, as well as antique ornaments and bric-a-brac, so that if, for instance, your hero is an expert on old silver you can describe Cellini Salts with confidence.

FLORA & FAUNA

I bought a hibiscus from Marks & Spencer recently. I'd seen photographs, but you can't beat the real thing. However, it is not practical nor even possible to grow a coconut palm in your garden, and that being so, a good photograph is the next best thing. Similarly, if either of your main characters is a zoologist it might not be advisable to borrow a gorilla or a giraffe from the local zoo, but have a good stock of pictures of them in their natural habitat, plus articles on their food and habits so that you can write knowledgeably about these things when you come to them. Reared on a diet of Tarzan films when young, I really did believe that crocodiles were vicious creatures who spent most of their lives rushing out at the unwary from their hiding places on river banks. Not so. They much prefer to be left alone and will swim away from trouble. Unless you happen to fall in the river right in the middle of them ... But we'll draw a veil over that one. And we've all seen *Jaws*, haven't we? Although I'm not prepared to put it to the test in the interests of veracity, I prefer to believe the deep-sea diver who wrote that most sharks are not aggressive. It's little gems like these that add richness to your store and swell the folders of cuttings. The only trouble is finding somewhere to keep them all, and a filing cabinet is not only useful but can often be bought second-hand, fairly cheaply, in office sales.

Finally, if in doubt about anything, go to the top. I once thought I'd like to set a book in a lighthouse. (No, I haven't done it yet, but I will one day.) Someone suggested I write to Trinity House for information and I did. A week later, the postman brought me an enormous envelope crammed with photographs of *every* lighthouse in the British Isles, and there are hundreds! If anyone wants to borrow any, do ask me, I've more than I need. My son decided to be an astronaut when he was twelve, wrote to NASA and received the most comprehensive material you could imagine. Literally dozens of glossy photographs, plus literature on space labs, technology, moon rockets (an astronaut hero? Mmm, there's an idea) and details of the workings of same. And, as I mentioned earlier, when I was setting a book in Finland I called in on the Finnish Consul in Manchester, who was quite charming, gave me coffee and biscuits and folders of photographs and information on his country. It's surprising what you get when you ask, so never be afraid to try. For the price of a phone call, or stamp, it's more than worth it. People are extremely helpful if approached in the right way, I've always found. Be brave. Pick up the phone, write that letter, buy that magazine.

You have nothing to lose but your ignorance.

Here's a brief list of useful books for all writers:

A good dictionary (Chambers or Oxford)
A synonym finder (Rodale, Collins, etc.)
The Writers' and Artists' Yearbook
The Oxford Dictionary for Writers and Editors
Familiar Quotations: John Bartlett
Dear Author: Michael Legat
An Author's Guide to Publishing: Michael Legat
Reader's Report: Christopher Derrick
Writing a Novel: John Braine
The Craft of Novel Writing: Dianne Doubtfire
Pen to Paper: Pamela Frankau
Confessions of a Story Teller: Paul Gallico
The Craft of Writing Romance: Jean Saunders
Writing Step By Step (to be published Spring 1988): Jean Saunders

FOURTEEN

All You Wanted To Know About Writing But Were Afraid To Ask

READING any instructional book is a one-way process. The reader can't suddenly stop and say, 'Hey, that's all very well, but –' With this in mind, I've set out below a lot of the questions that have been asked me and other romantic novelists over the past few years, many of which keep recurring.

1. How can I write about steely-eyed, attractive tycoons when there are so few (if any) in real life?

It's precisely because they are thin on the ground that they become so important in women's fiction. Let's face it, we all have our fantasies. Isn't it wonderful that you can legitimately indulge your fantasies for the enjoyment of others? And get paid! Refer to the chapter on heroes for more precise details.

2. How can I cope with that dreadful mental block that occurs some mornings just before – or even just after – I have started to write?

It will make you feel a lot better, I'm sure, to know that this happens to *all* writers at some time, and to some more frequently than others. It happens to me at least twice in every book I write. I'll tell you first how I've coped with it, and then some of the tips I have picked up from my fellow writers along the way. First, I'll get up, make a cup of coffee, take the dog for a run, or even, in extremis, clean the kitchen floor. But – before I do all that, I've mentally consigned the problem to my subconscious (i.e. George the Automatic Pilot in the back of every writer's brain. Have you ever noticed that you can often go to bed with some unresolved problem whirling about in your brain, and when you wake up in the morning, the solution has come to you? That's George who's been at work overnight).

So after half an hour – an hour maybe – I get back to my desk, and that little mental and physical break is usually enough to enable me to look with fresh eyes upon the manuscript. If this doesn't work for you and you are still staring at that virgin sheet with a mind as blank, take half a day off from *that* book and *write something totally different* – the letters you have been putting off, your diary, perhaps, or copy one of your favourite poems out – you will still be engaged in the writing process, which is important, and when you return to your magnum opus, all will be well.

Other writers garden, cook, go shopping, go for a walk or ring their friends and say 'Help!' – that's happened to me too – but always with the knowledge that the block will pass. If none of these work, please consider seriously whether you are writing the correct book at that time. Perhaps it would be better to put it completely to one side – and begin another. I have done this at least three times, coming back to the book six months or so later – even, in one case, eighteen months – and it was ready to be written. I had just begun the book at the wrong time for me.

3. How much preparatory work should I do before I start my book?

This is a question frequently asked by beginners. The simple answer is: as much as you want – but don't let it all show. I'll explain that. Research can be so enjoyable for some people that it becomes an increasingly attractive alternative to actual writing. Ages ago, a friend of mine (who shall be nameless) embarked on detailed research for a romantic historical novel set against a background of the Boxer Rebellion in China. She became so fascinated and engrossed in the research that the novel was never written, but she now knows more about the Boxer Rebellion than any except the most learned specialist in this field. So be warned. Don't get carried away by your research. To be realistic, if you are setting your romantic novel on a tropical island in the Caribbean, by all means make it an imaginary one, but check the flora and fauna of that area, also the industries, climate, types of houses people have, and so on – and of course, the people themselves. (You might want to write about a family of Chinese traders living on a Caribbean island, but it might be considered an unlikely setting for them.) One vital essential is that you do not burden your reader with all your knowledge – you convey subtly the atmosphere of that place (or period, if historical) and your reader does the rest with her own imagination. A friend of mine once read an historical novel set in a certain period because she wanted details of that period for her own use, and she was surprised to find how few actual hard facts there were. Yet the atmosphere was totally convincing. Do not *tell* all you have researched, but convey it gently.

4. How much should I listen to the advice of others in connection with my writing?

If there is within you a burning desire to write something, and it is so strong that nothing will stop you, go ahead, because you will probably have a real cracker on your hands. But this marvellous intensity does not, alas, happen all the time, and you may need a little guidance. At this point then, it is important to distinguish well-meaning but amateur advice from that of a professional. For example, if an editor sends you a detailed criticism of your work, first, congratulations, because it is obviously worthy of criticism, and believe me, editors don't do that for everyone because they don't have time; and second, read it thoroughly, absorb it and act on it. You may not agree. You may think you've written the best thing since *Gone With The Wind*, but you haven't or she would have accepted immediately with shrieks of joy.

If you join the Romantic Novelists' Association as a probationer (i.e. one who has never had a full-length romantic novel accepted) you will be asked to submit one novel a year, which will be criticised by experts. That will be a professionally objective criticism from someone with no particular axe to grind. A personal note here: when I joined the Romantic Novelists' Association in 1970 their reader was Helen MacGregor. As I've already said, her criticisms – which I have still, together with her letters – were extremely valuable to me. She was a marvellous critic and a wonderful woman, and when she died recently left behind literally hundreds of friends. I owe her a great debt.

In short, you don't have to *act* upon the advice of anyone, but would be well advised to listen at least to the points they make. It's your book, after all.

5. How do I avoid dating my book via fashions, slang, and prices of things, etcetera?

A tricky one this. The answer is to avoid specifics, such as 'She wore a mini skirt; he said, "It's fab/brill/super." She said, "Yes, and it only cost me two pounds."' An extreme and dramatic example of all three in one sentence, but very relevant. With regard to fashion, be sufficiently vague in your reference to style so that the reader can 'see' it in current fashion, as thus: 'She bought herself a dress for the party, swirly blues and greens in a soft silky material.' Avoid slang. Avoid mentioning specific amounts of money – for example, if the heroine buys a car: 'He told her the price and she raised her eyebrows. It was more than she wanted to pay, but she could just afford it.' No details. Your reader will convert that to contemporary prices. (Similarly, be vague about the model of the car.)

6. Can I have a new kind of heroine? I'm a bit bored with the old ones. Can she be more intelligent, up-market, and experienced?

This could be answered in one word: Yes! But that would be dodging the genuine concern behind the question. Every heroine is, or should be, different – much of that is discussed elsewhere – but I appreciate the point this question makes. While I wrote each one of my books, that heroine was, to me, totally different from any that had gone before. She was new to me. All my heroines may have had certain similarities, but these shared

qualities were the very features that made them individuals –
their independence, their strong-mindedness, their determination
to *be* individuals and not pale shadows of someone else or to be
forced into any mould. So I will say to this questioner – have
your heroine that university don, that racing driver, that
advertising executive. Have her experienced – without being
specific – and it may well work beautifully for you. You will not
know until you try. The writing game is full of new creations
and characters who are completely different from anything that
has gone before, and isn't it marvellous that this should be so?

7. I always have problems about the starting point of my book. Is it advisable to use, as a jumping-off point, a complete change in my heroine's life?

This, if you have done your research, is where you will find most
romantic novelists begin. The heroine going to a new job, a new
country – or both, inheriting a sufficient sum of money to
change her life style; being forced to go somewhere totally
unexpected by circumstances beyond her control; or by the hero
entering her life and causing chaos. It is in this very change that
the challenge lies. If you don't have this, you have a book which
could have started at any point, and there is not as much impact.
In fact most novels, not just romantic novels, are initiated by
some change, major or minor, which sparks off the events of the
novel.

8. I've always read that conflict is vital to a romantic novel, how do I go about introducing it?

First of all, a lot of conflict lies in the characters themselves (i.e.
hero and heroine) and the effect they have on each other, but
there must be a flashpoint to trigger off this clash of personalities
and sustain it throughout the book. Remember the woman who
said to me 'I love it where they fight all the way through.' Yes,
well, we have to give them good reason to fight all the way
through, don't we? So here are just a few examples taken from
my own books. I'm sure you'll think of as many more again –
from all sources.

Black Niall: Hero returns to small Scottish village after years away, intent on buying heroine's large house for a hotel, in face of her opposition partly fired by an old family feud.

The Man at La Valaise: English journalist heroine kidnapped by Russian in South of France and held incommunicado because she witnessed a Russian defector. The conflict lies in her attempts to escape.

The Dark Isle: Heroine's opposition to hero's television team in an effort to preserve the privacy of the island from documentary exposure.

There are literally dozens more. Regard the conflict as the spark that keeps the book alive for you. Believe me, it's easier to write a cracking good row than a conversation where both hero and heroine are being nice to each other – though, on reflection, when those nice bits follow a sustained battle, they can be very sweet, and *extremely* interesting!

9. I have problems keeping my characters in order. How on earth can I control them?

It's very difficult when a minor character 'takes off' and becomes stronger and more assertive than he/she should be. I sympathise with this one because it's happened not only to me but to most of my romantic-novelist friends. The answer, alas, lies in a bit of rewriting. Stop immediately you realise what is happening, go back and *ruthlessly* prune his/her speech, actions, mannerisms. Then take a deep breath, and vow not to let it happen again. In *Snow on the Hills* I had a rather sexy gardener. (No, his name wasn't Mellors.) He began to get far too interesting, so I had to do as above, prune him out a bit, and keep a firm grip on him afterwards. He soon settled down. This is one of the rare occasions I have had to rewrite several pages but it was worth it. And talking of rewriting, see the next question.

10. How much rewriting do authors have to do?

As little or as much as is necessary. In the case of most successful romantic novelists with a totally professional attitude, very little. We have such a clear picture in our minds before we start that it goes down on paper much as it will be in that final draft to the publisher. If *you* can see it vividly, so will your reader. If you can't, how can you expect her to? If you've read this book properly so far, you should know what you are about to do *before* you even start the book, and only the occasional repetition of a word will have to be altered (with the help of your trusty book of synonyms).

Don't forget that with each rewriting, some of the life and fire is taken out of your manuscript. Keep it. It is very precious.

11. How can I create credible plot situations?

How credible do you want them to be? Remember that a lot of fiction, and not only the romantic variety, does depend on its power to make the reader suspend his/her disbelief. If you want to write novels with bags of realism, poverty, kitchen-sink drama, wife-beatings, incest and other subjects that comprise a great part of any daily newspaper, don't let me stop you; write them. But they won't be romantic novels, will they? And that's what we're talking about now.

If by credible you mean believable, surely there is nothing unbelievable about a young woman obtaining a post as governess to a wealthy man; a young woman having an inheritance; or starting a new life in a new country; or resisting the attempts of someone to change her neat, ordered existence? These things can – indeed do – all happen.

You want your heroine to get stranded on a desert island where – surprise, surprise – there is a male castaway? Great. That has happened too. There have even been *true* books written about such experiences. Just go ahead and write what you want to, however fantastic it may seem, because, somewhere, it may have happened, and someone is going to love it, because we all need our dreams, and if you can write about *my* fantasies sufficiently well, I'll look forward to reading *your* book.

12. When I am writing sexy scenes, I feel inhibited. Why?

It's the old, old question. What you really mean is, you worry about what your mother/aunt/granny/old teacher is going to think and whether they will be shocked, don't you? It happens to every new writer. The answer is to accept the fact that they *will* probably be shocked, surprised, dismayed and wonder how a nice girl like you could write such things. In all walks of life too many people spend too much time worrying about what others will think or say about their behaviour. If you let this fear inhibit you, you might as well never write at all, because somebody – even if only an editor – is going to read your book, and they might not approve. Writing, unlike art, is a mass-consumption business. An artist or a musician can demonstrate their skill to a small circle of friends. Writers by definition want to get into print for large audiences. So stop looking fearfully over your shoulder. As a final solution, you can always write under a pen name – and don't tell Aunt Mabel. Hundreds of writers do, for a variety of reasons. They just get used to answering to two – or more – different names when they are amongst their fellow writers.

It's not only to sexy scenes that this inhibition applies. You are putting a part of yourself into everything you write, exposing your mind for others to see. If you didn't do this, you would have a dull book, completely impersonal. If it's any consolation, it gets easier as you go along. You'll stop worrying about it after the second or third book, honest.

13. What do you think about writers' circles?

If the circle is a working group, it's valuable. If it's a talking group, take care. Many writers' circles simply provide an opportunity for ego-trips. Some are excellent, but you won't discover which kind until you have attended a few times. A well-known journalist, Jill Dick, has compiled a book listing writers' circles in Great Britain. It is periodically updated and is readily available from her at 'Oldacre', Horderns Park Road, Chapel-en-le-Frith, Derbyshire SK12 68Y: please send £1.85 and a large stamped addressed envelope.

14. I'm sometimes tempted by the adverts for correspondence courses in writing. Do you think they represent value for money?

Correspondence courses need treating with care. The more reputable offer good tuition often until you are published (or your money back). Many novice writers make the mistake of thinking that the act of taking the course will guarantee their success as a writer. This is not so. There is no substitute for work. Correspondence courses in all fields report a high drop-out rate. But if you are prepared to read the lessons, submit the assignments, take note of the criticism, and learn from your mistakes, then you can benefit.

15. Are there organisations to help romantic novelist beginners?

I recommend any determined beginner to join the Romantic Novelists' Association as a probationer (i.e. unpublished). You should write initially (with s.a.e., please) to: Marina Oliver, 'Half Hidden', West Lane, Bledlow, Nr Princes Risborough, Buckinghamshire HP17 9PF. The conditions of membership for the novice is that you submit one complete romance novel annually – therefore it makes you work. The novel will be read, and, if it is of publishable standard, forwarded to a suitable publisher. If not up to publication quality you will get it back with a detailed criticism. I recommend any beginner to join. I received a great deal of help from them for which I will always be grateful.

16. I've heard mention of writers' conferences many times. Do many romantic novelists attend, and would they be of help to me?

Yes – and yes. First, let's define what we mean by conferences. There are one-day seminars, weekend conferences, and longer schools. The pattern of these tends to be similar in that there are experienced guest speakers on many types of writing, discussion groups and possibly small tutorial sessions. On the informal side you will meet (and to me this is equally valuable) many successful people from all over the country, and from all branches of writing. One of the writer's big problems is loneliness – so the level of talk at these conferences is highly intense. Be prepared to come home afterwards absolutely exhausted – but with the writing batteries recharged. I can give you the addresses of two:

the Scarborough Writers' Weekend has been running very successfully since 1973, twice a year, in April and in November. The Secretary is Audrey Wilson, The Firs, Filey Road, Osgodby, Scarborough, Yorkshire. The Swanwick Writers' Summer School lasts six days, takes place in August each year, and the Secretary is Philippa Boland, The Red House, Mardens Hill, Crowborough, Sussex TN6 1XN.

There are many more, of course, but I don't know the names of the secretaries, sorry – but once you've been to one, you'll soon find out on the grapevine. I just don't have time to go to more than two, as a general rule, unless I'm asked to speak.

17. I'm fed up with writing 'he said' and 'she said'. Any suggestions?

Yes. He (or she):

added	explained	proclaimed	sneered
agreed	gasped	promised	squeaked
answered	grumbled	protested	squealed
argued	implored	quavered	stammered
averred	invited	queried	stated
babbled	interrupted	questioned	stormed
blurted out	jeered	rejoined	stressed
breathed	joked	remarked	stuttered
burst out	lamented	repeated	swore
butted in	maintained	responded	taunted
commanded	moaned	retaliated	teased
commented	mocked	retorted	thundered
complained	mouthed	returned	urged
conceded	mumbled	revealed	uttered
confessed	murmured	riposted	vowed
contended	muttered	scoffed	wailed
continued	objected	scorned	went on
declared	observed	screamed	whimpered
demanded	opined	shouted	whined
drawled	ordered	shrieked	whispered
echoed	parried	sighed	yelled.
enquired	persisted	snorted	
exclaimed	prattled	sobbed	

Are those enough?

18. How can I describe my characters in a more colourful way?

By using your imagination. By *seeing* the picture you wish to create before putting it down on paper. There are ways of describing things that state the bare essentials but don't put any images in your reader's mind, and there are other ways of saying the same thing that will create a vivid picture or enable the reader to *see* what you mean. You'd like a few examples? Okay, here goes.

You could say:	*Or you could say this:*
He was very tall.	He had to duck his head as he came through the doorway.
He looked tired.	He sank wearily into a chair and closed his eyes.
He looked very aggressive, and tough, and she didn't like him.	There was an arrogant, hackle-raising confidence about him that made prickles stir on the back of her neck.
She wasn't sure whether he was annoyed or amused.	His wide mouth appeared to be twitching, whether with anger or suppressed laughter it was impossible to say.
His eyes were cold.	His eyes were of a cold brilliance that made her shiver.
She was attractive, and used to men's glances, but she didn't like the way he was looking at her.	She was well used to men weighing her up and down, in street or shop, just about everywhere she went, but it didn't mean that she had to like it. She had developed a cool, dismissive gaze. She used it now on the man whose dark eyes were scanning her as if searching for hidden weapons.

| She didn't want to listen to him any more; she felt tired and weak – and tearful. | She put her hands to her ears, tears of tiredness and weakness filling her eyes and spilling out down her cheeks, and her soft golden hair tumbled about her face as she shook her head helplessly. |

Those in the left column are fine – but the ones in the right one are better. If you see what is happening you will be able to describe it more vividly.

19. Are competitions of any value, or are they only promotional stunts?

There must be literally dozens of competitions for writers, every year, and these are widely advertised in writer's publications. The Betty Trask award for a romantic or traditonal novel was launched last year, and with a top prize of £12,000, is it worth it? Are you kidding? But that's the top one. There are many lesser ones well worth trying for. Some publishers occasionally run them as a talent-spotting exercise. The rewards may not be as great but you could find yourself launched on a career as romantic novelist before you can say 'paperback rights'! So keep your eyes open. Even short-story competitions in women's magazines are useful as a launching pad. I've never won any, but as I've never entered any, that's hardly surprising. Best of luck!

20. What is meant by the term vanity publishing?

The simple answer to this one is that you will pay to be published instead of being paid by a reputable publisher. Do I recommend it? No (see Chapter 12, 'Meet Your Publisher ...'). But as long as you know that this is what is involved, the choice is yours. If you have a couple of thousand pounds to spare, and the desperate urge to see your name on the cover of your book, and it has already been rejected several times, why not publish it yourself? There are many printers in Yellow Pages who will quote you prices, but expect to do your own marketing, advertising, and general promotion as well as deliveries. It will keep you slim if nothing else. On a more serious note, save your money, save your time, keep on writing. The next one may well succeed on its own merits.

FIFTEEN

Blueprint For Success

YOU want to write? Of course you do, or you wouldn't be reading this book. You want to succeed in your writing? What have you learnt from this book? That you have to be motivated, enthusiastic, and organised. You must love words, be intensely curious about everything that is going on around you – and have the imagination to do something with those images. And when you begin writing you will have to learn to take criticism – but with an optimistic frame of mind. You will need to do research, of course, and, finally, it will be necessary to concentrate wholly on what you are doing. So let's go through all these points one by one, taking as the first the most important one of all:

1. Motivation

Unless you are motivated, there is no point in beginning anything, whether it be painting, sculpting, mountain climbing, marathon running – or writing. Unless you want to write that book more than anything else you won't do it. It sounds so obvious, but it's not to some writers who moan that they *ought* to be writing but there are so many other things to do first. Fine. Go and do those other things if that's what you prefer. No one in the world can force you to write if you don't want to.

If you happen to be employed on a production line in a factory then you are an essential part of a larger chain and you *must* be there, and if you can't be, someone else *must* do that work instead of you. But writing? Ah, that's different. It is an individual and entirely personal thing. It is you. A dictionary definition of motive is: concerned with the initiation of action. Put more simply, unless you are motivated, you cannot begin. So get to it!

2. Enthusiasm

All the world loves an enthusiast. Their love of life – and of their subjects – is totally infectious. Watch Patrick Moore on *The Sky at Night* when he is discussing astronomy, or David Bellamy on the subject of botany – enthusiasm shines out.

Enthusiasts communicate well because they are so engrossed in their passions, whether these be tropical fish, kite flying, or Chinese brasses, that they make us interested in these subjects as well. In the same way, publishers, editors and readers will respond to the enthusiasm you bring to your writing, because there is a freshness shining through the words that is very appealing.

Why are so many romantic writers women? It is because women are generally far more romantic than men in their outlook on life, and it is this *belief* in romance which comes across so successfully in their writing. So get excited about your work from the outset – no, even before you begin, when those ideas are still bubbling about in your brain. Be there, feel your character's problems as your own. Live the book. Love it. *Be* it.

3. Organisation

I've said somewhere else in this book that writers lead lives of total chaos. True. In part. Edna Ferber summed it up beautifully when she said: 'Clothes are unimportant. Teeth go unfilled … you are cradled in a white paper cocoon, tied up with typewriter ribbon.' In other words, everything else about you can be falling into total disarray and very probably is, but in your writing, have your mind organised. First there is the mental discipline, second there are the tools for the job. You will have set aside your time for writing, you will have cleared the old newspapers, cats, Aunt Minnie's fluffy squeaking parrot off your desk, and there it waits for you. You will then have set out your pens and paper (or typewriter and paper), dictionary and book of synonyms within easy reach, and you are ready to begin for the day. That is being organised. If you find, ten minutes after you begin your writing, that you have forgotten some small essential tool of the trade (eraser, carbon paper, or whatever) then you are not organised, and your concentration (see point 10) will suffer, and so will your writing.

My advice, which is quite simple, is this: make a list of all you need in your day's writing and pin it up on the wall near your work table. It will soon become force of habit to check your list and mentally tick off each item before you begin. You will be organised!

4. Words

Crenellated battlements – curvaceous – crackling – shimmering – ululate – undulate – charisma – chimera – screech – shriek – scratching – shushing – shivering – simmering – voluptuous – cacophony – crescendo – chrysanthemum – prestidigitator – pippistrelle – treacle – creakily – dulcimer – enchantment – cantankerous – sensuality – serendipity. Words. If you don't love words you will never be a writer. Writers collect words. I collected those, and I have a few thousand more that I love the sound of, but I'm not going to tell you. Go and collect your own. I didn't even know what crenellated meant when I first started my fairy stories in the long ago, but I fell in love with it and so I used it – although it does help, when you are a mature adult, to know what the words mean that you use! Words are the first tool of a writer's trade. Enjoy them, say them out loud, use them well. Write what you want to say as clearly as possible. Don't write sentences of such profound obscurity that your reader is obliged to re-read them with furrowed brow as she tries to sort out exactly what you mean. She will be irritated, and she will end up skipping bits that look as though they require an 'A' level in English Literature to comprehend, and she won't buy your next book. Straightforward prose can convey subtleties of meaning far better than obscure, muddied words. If in doubt, read out loud what you have written, or get a friend to read it for you. Or speak into a tape-recorder and then play it back. You may get a shock. Or you may be delighted. If you would like to read something that is totally incomprehensible to *everybody*, get hold of a VAT information booklet that is designed to help VAT payers know what is going on. But keep the aspirin bottle handy; you'll need it.

5. Curiosity

Or the gentle art of snooping. Eavesdropping plays a large part in the life of any writer. The ability to 'tune out' your ears to what is going on in the way of conversation at your own dinner table in a restaurant, and 'tune in', like some form of radar, to that which is taking place at a nearby table, is a talent to be acquired with all possible speed, if you haven't already mastered it. This must not be confused with nosiness for its own sake, which is, of course, abhorrent. It is more a kind of material gathering for future reference. Aren't people fascinating? If you answer no to that one, forget about being a writer. But you haven't. Listen and watch what is going on around you everywhere you go. Sit on one of those seats they have dotted all around shopping centres and watch people pass. I guarantee you'll see not only lots of minor characters for your books, but quite a few potential heroines. Heroes? Alas, very few of those – which is why, my dears, romantic novels sell so well. There are so few gloriously virile, six-foot-four males with steely grey eyes around that we have to make them up. Or maybe they just don't frequent shopping centres. Perhaps we should form a network of men-watchers in the same way as ornithologists do with birds. Sightings would be reported, romantic novelists would gather, notebooks and cameras at the ready, another specimen would be duly recorded for posterity, and one bewildered male would wonder at his sudden fame. And he would never know why ...

6. Imagination

With a limited imagination it might be possible for you to become a journalist. Difficult, but possible, if for instance you wrote strictly factual articles on, say, stamp-collecting, pot-plants, the organisation of laundrettes. You would need a certain facility with words, facts at your fingertips, and away you would go.

There is no possible way you will ever be a writer of fiction without a rich and fertile imagination. How many times have writers of romantic fiction heard the cry from some despairing beginner: 'Oh, it's all right for you, but I lead such a *very quiet life.*' The italics are mine. What do they think romantic novelists do? Personal research on hundreds of men to find the ideal hero? The mind boggles. We'd never have time to actually write if that were the case. What the successful novelist of any genre possesses is an abundant fantasy world in her (or his) head. She may live in Morecambe with elderly parents, she may never have married, perhaps never have been intimately associated with any man – there are several successful romantic novelists to whom this description could apply, whose books have caused palpitations in readers' breasts all over the world. It doesn't make a great deal of difference in the long run because what these women have been able to do is translate their vivid fantasies into words on paper, to weave spells that capture their readers' own imaginations and lead them into the world of hero and heroine and conflict galore. 'The child nurtured on fantasy does not despise real woods because he has read of enchanted woods; rather the reading makes all woods enchanted.' C.S. Lewis wrote that long ago, and it is as true today as it was then. We can all remember the childhood games of cowboys and Indians, dragons and monsters, princesses locked up in towers waiting to be rescued by the prince; remember too all those lovely bedtime stories which took us into realms of gold. We carry this faculty into adulthood but are often less ready to indulge it, perhaps because we do not connect it with those childhood dreams. Yet in our reading we still give full rein to our imagination. Television has not replaced this enjoyment, as some people once feared. Admittedly it does all the work for us, and reading is a personal, solitary pleasure. When your reader is enjoying the romantic novel you have written, you and she are sharing something unique because no two readers see a book in exactly the same way. There's food for thought!

So, what is your responsibility as a writer in the imagination stakes? It is to create a stimulating plot with sufficient originality to hold your reader's interest and imagination; to have it unfold through the characters you have convincingly drawn; against a background that will take her into the realms of her particular fantasy. It is a threefold task. In the words of the old song 'imagination is funny ...'.

Upon your ability to conjure up and project through your writing rests the success of your storytelling. This is a much neglected facility, but let's face it, a writer *is* a storyteller. Be a good one while you are about it. It is too easy to lose sight of that aim in a world of literary themes and pretentious clap-trap. You want to tell a story? Go ahead and do it. Many great writers have regarded themselves first and foremost as storytellers – and what's wrong with that?

7. Criticism

'To avoid criticism, do nothing, say nothing, be nothing.' So wrote Elbert Hubbard, a writer of whom I must confess I had never heard before, but he certainly summed it up beautifully. The ability to accept criticism is not something that comes easily to most of us, for the simple reason that what we have written is the precious product of our own mind and we feel a great deal of affection for it – naturally enough – and if someone pulls a face and says that they don't really like it, it hurts. Of course it hurts! Both our feelings and our pride, not necessarily in that order. Hurt feelings can be repaired, and pride can be swallowed. I've done enough of both to know what I'm talking about. But it's what you do next that counts, and here is what I advise: unruffle your feathers, sit down and take a long, cool, objective look at the criticism, then re-read your words in as impartial a manner as you can, and you may find, much to your astonishment, that the critic was right. It takes courage to admit it, but if, after that detached assessment of his/her words you can say, yes, I see their point, you will have learned a valuable lesson, and you will have a more professional attitude as a result.

I have been to many writers' circles and sat in on manuscript evenings, and have heard fair criticisms given – and joined in myself – of the members' work. I have also seen the expressions on the faces of some recipients, and heard their words as they either leapt fiercely to the defence of what they had written, or nodded and said, slowly perhaps, 'Hmm, I see what you mean.'

The latter had got it, the ability to accept.

There are geniuses (or should it be genii?) about, who *know* that every word they write is *perfect*. This book is not addressed to them, it is addressed to you, and you are a normal human being with human faults and failings, like me. We all need help at the beginning. Please learn how to accept that assistance with grace.

8. Optimism

It is not easy to remain cool and calm when the washer has just flooded the kitchen floor, the kettle has given a despairing 'pop' and refused to heat the water for your much-needed cup of tea, and next door's hamster, who you are looking after for a week, has gnawed his way to freedom and escaped into the garage to hide among the accumulated debris of several years. It is just as difficult to keep a sunny smile on your face when the postman has brought you an ominously familiar envelope with your handwriting on it, back from the publisher.

If you are a pessimist your reaction to this series of disasters will undoubtedly be one of: 'I *knew* it, these things always happen to me', accompanied by a frantic wringing of hands which won't do any good at all either for washer, kettle, hamster or yourself. The optimist gives vent to a few choice expletives, mops up the water, thus cleaning the kitchen floor at the same time (saving herself a job later), mends the fuse and makes her cup of tea, lays an interesting trail of food back to the cage to lure Harry Hamster out from wherever it is he's hiding, and then gets on with her writing because she knows that all these trials and tribulations are but temporary setbacks in the glorious game of life. And she's already made up her mind that her next book will be accepted anyway.

Be optimistic. You can look on the dark side or you can look on the bright side and, believe it, bright is much better. Think positive. Tell yourself that you know you are about to succeed, that success is just around the corner and it very probably will be.

9. Research

A writer is like a sponge. Even though we may be unaware of

the process, from an early age we are absorbing impressions, of places, people, and events, and storing them away for future reference. But we need not be solely dependent on personal experiences as we have a vast treasure store of information upon which we can call. Books, newspapers, magazines, libraries, television and films all supply us with an endless stream of material. Too much material. Our task then is to select what is required for our needs, and this is the process we call research. If too much shows it will smother the story. You must never tell all you know, but what you don't say will – or should – be communicated in your writing. In the confidence of your storytelling lies the secret of successful research. When Margaret Mitchell wrote *Gone With The Wind*, one of the greatest love stories of all time, she created a scale model of the city of Atlanta for one small part of the book to get her setting absolutely right. And incidentally it is said that she wrote the first chapter *seventy* times!

Don't think that the reader is going to go through your book with a fine-tooth comb seeking out inaccuracies, but equally, don't insult her intelligence by having your heroine, for example, travelling by underground railway in Rome or Manchester. Edgar Rice Burroughs knew so little about Africa that he featured tigers in an early Tarzan book. (No, I didn't know that there weren't any there, either, until someone told me.)

Be warned, though, that research can be so fascinating that it may become a substitute for writing. Don't let that happen. Enough and no more should be your watchword. One famous writer is reputed to have said: 'Write now, research later!' He certainly had a point.

10. Concentration

Get the blinkers on and concentrate on what you are doing to the exclusion of everything else. I was once writing a very important love scene in my fifth book, *Laird of Gaela*, when my children were young. Not only were they young, but they were on holiday from school. Not only were they on holiday but they each had two friends visiting. And not only all those things – but it was *raining. And they were all playing in the house.* Was I downhearted? Well, yes, but it only made me the more determined to get on with what I had to do. The urge to write something so strong that it's almost coming out of your pores is a very effective aid to concentration and withdrawal from the rest of the world. I was on the point of having my hero and heroine fog-bound in an icy house for the night. Alone. With fuel for the fire and only one mattress upon which to sleep. I *had* to know what happened next. Wouldn't *you* be curious too?

'Right,' I said to the six grubby, wide-eyed infants. 'I have to write. It is very important. Play all over the house but keep out of the study, and only shout me if it's an emergency – understand?' Six heads nodded. Giggles were hastily stifled. They still think I'm crazy, but at least I'm used to it now. Off I went, leaving biscuits and orange juice at the ready in the kitchen. For the next three hours, while the rain drummed steadily and unceasingly on the windows, I wrote. Herds of mini-elephants thundered up and down the stairs, wild Red-Indian shrieks rent the air, and I wrote, locked away in my own little world on a Scottish island with thick mist swirling round the large old manor house and a throbbing sexual tension effectively building up between my two main characters, Jago Black and Tara Blaine. I was only so distantly aware of the noise that it scarcely impinged on my consciousness. The scene was one of the best in the book (she said modestly). *That*'s concentration.

As a footnote to the Blueprint for Success, remember how childhood days were overshadowed by constant admonitions, mainly dos and don'ts? And mainly to do with finishing up all your nice rice pudding/cabbage/prunes because somewhere out there were poor children who would be very grateful for said portions?

The following dos and don'ts are not of that kind, you will be relieved to know. These *will* be good for you. Let's begin with the don'ts.

Don't be obscure. Say what you want to say as clearly as possible.

Don't talk about your ideas. They will vanish like mist in the morning sunlight if you do. Get them onto paper. Let nothing interfere with that precious transition from *your* fantasy to *your* book.

Don't write a book that is 80,000 words long when an editor has asked for one of 55,000. She didn't say it for fun. She said it for very practical reasons to do with publishing requirements, printers, paper and other costings that you wot not of, and you'll have to do a hell of a lot of pruning which will serve you right.

Don't throw away old manuscripts. Keep them, read them again six months, a year, even five years later. You may be pleasantly surprised to find that there are possibilities in some that can be used, with rewriting; characters, ideas, settings, etc. If you had discarded them you would have totally forgotten about them.

Don't make a pest of yourself, once you have sent a manuscript off, by telephoning or writing to the publishers every five minutes to see what they are doing with your precious book, because they'll parcel it up and bung it back. They have lots of work to do, you see. Forget about it. Get on with the next one and when you send them that it will jog their memories nicely and they'll decide you are a hard worker, and perhaps be impressed.

Don't introduce too many characters all at once. It confuses the reader. Have you ever been to a party and been introduced to ten or more people in quick succession? You have? Then you'll know exactly what I mean.

Don't rewrite too many times and take all the life out of your book. There is a lovely freshness in a first writing that is destroyed by constant alterations. Do only what is necessary.

Don't listen to the prophets of doom, the depressors, who are at any gathering of writers or would-be writers and who look at you sadly and say things like: 'You're wasting your time, you know. *I've* been trying for *years* and have not got anywhere.' If their writing is anything like their talking, is that any surprise? Move smartly away and save both time and temper. They are not worth arguing with.

Don't be beaten by rejection. John Creasey had a total of 742 rejections for various works before he succeeded. He wasn't defeated, was he? And he clearly didn't take any notice of the prophets of doom in the previous paragraph.

Don't be timid. Be yourself. You are unique. No one has ever said or written before *exactly* what you are saying or writing. The world may be waiting to hear *you*. Be bold. Go ahead and say it. You have nothing to lose, except an inferiority complex.

Don't go to all the trouble of having your precious typescript beautifully bound for sending to a publisher, because they'll only have to take it to bits to read it and send it to the printer. The simplest way to send it is in a large wallet-type folder or even in the box which contained the typing paper. They'll heave a sigh of relief if you do so — always providing you have numbered your pages, of course!

Now for the dos.

Do keep at least one copy of everything you send off to a publisher. Things do get lost in the post occasionally, or even (whisper it softly) at a publishing house. It seems too obvious to say, but you'd be surprised how many people have not heeded that advice — and have had to rewrite an entire book.

Do use the method of writing most suited to you. Mine is with black pen on A4-size lined paper. I am happy with that. You may prefer to write in red crayon on cartridge paper, or in a teeny notebook, old diary, or on the backs of envelopes. Fine. As long as you remember to get it neatly typed when it's done so that a publisher can read it. That's what counts, not how it first came into being from your mind.

Do remember that there is no new thing under the sun. You just have to find a different way of saying things that have been said a thousand times before, since storytelling first began in the caves of our forefathers.

Do believe in yourself, for if you don't how can you expect anyone else to do so?

Do write every day if humanly possible. That lovely thread of continuity that keeps your characters and story alive is very precious, and daily writing will keep it strong.

Do have a set of rules to which you adhere as part of your personal writing discipline. If you decide, for instance, that you will write every evening from ten o'clock to midnight, your brain will become accustomed to so doing, and will be raring to go as time draws near. And, yes, you can bend those rules occasionally. You can start at nine if you like!

Do read a lot in between writing your books. You will be delving into other writers' minds, drawing on the rich store of imagination – you will *be* part of the wonderful world of books.

Do be helpful and co-operative with your publisher. There are temperamental authors and there are non-temperamental authors. With which kind do you think your publisher prefers to deal?

Do be professional, both in the presentation of your manuscript and in your attitude. A writer who gets paid for his/her writing is a professional. So is the publisher. If you have a deadline, deliver the goods (i.e. the book) on or before that date, not six months afterwards. And make sure it is neatly typed, double-spaced on the size of paper he prefers (if in doubt, ask). He'll be pleased, and a happy publisher is one who will look kindly upon your future work, which all helps to oil the wheels, doesn't it?

Do love your characters while you are writing about them. If you don't then you're wasting your time and should be doing something else. If you care about them sufficiently, this will be conveyed to your reader and she will want to find out what happens to them, and be keen to read your next book as well.

Do watch out for changing trends in the kind of books you are writing. You may want to be a trend-setter, to boldly go where no writer has gone before. Fine, if you've written fifty and been a best-seller for fifteen years or more, not so fine if this is your first book. If you're a new girl in an office you don't march in on your first day and begin reorganising, do you? Not if you possess a grain of common sense, you don't. Try your bold, trend-setting book when you're more experienced, say after you have twenty published. And good luck with it. The world needs people like you.

SIXTEEN

A Writer's Scrapbook

Sit back and relax, you're going on a ride. I make no apologies for what follows. Just as some people collect scraps of cloth in different textures, colours and patterns to make a beautiful patchwork quilt, over the years, in like fashion, I've accumulated a rag-bag of literary scraps, thoughts and ideas for my own entertainment – and inspiration. See what effect they have on you, beginning with my favourites on writing.

Logan Pearsall Smith: What I like in a good author is not what he says, but what he whispers.

Ursula Le Guin: There have been great societies that did not use the wheel, but there have been no societies that did not tell stories.

Erma Bombeck: Why I'm a writer: I'm too old for a paper round, too young for Social Security, too tired for an affair, and too clumsy to steal.

Pliny the Younger: Too much polishing weakens rather than improves a work.

Henry James: Summer afternoon – summer afternoon; to me those have always been the two most beautiful words in the English language.

Margaret Atwood: Why do I write? I think the real question is: 'Why doesn't everyone?'

Christopher Lehmann-Haupt: You don't learn to write by reading books on how to write. You learn by groping in the dark with your pencil or typewriter, until you've hit on something a little bit better than what you've written before.

Pat Leimbach: There is a maximum of five free hours in a housewife/writer/mother's day — they lie between midnight and five a.m. ... [How true! M.W.]

Desiderius Erasmus: When I get a little money, I buy books; and if any is left, I buy food and clothes.

Henry David Thoreau: This world is but canvas to our imaginations.

Raymond Chandler: Literature is any sort of writing that reaches a sufficient intensity of performance to glow with its own heat.

Franklin Field: The great dividing line between success and failure can be expressed in five little words — I did not have time.

Katherine Anne Porter: If you want to write a novel about mountaineering, all you have to do is climb *one* mountain — part way.

And the final words on writing come from an author, alas anonymous, to his editor upon delivering his book manuscript: 'I've got 80,000 words, but I'm not sure if they're the right 80,000.' We all know that feeling, don't we?

There's more. There's lots more. Still sitting comfortably? I heard this gem recently on television. 'Whatever women do, they must do twice as well as men to be thought half as good. Fortunately, *this is not difficult*.' I wrote it down immediately in my little red book. Not the thoughts of Chairman Mao, but a battered notebook I bought years ago and began writing in the snippets I enjoyed reading, from papers, magazines and, oh yes, the notice boards outside churches. They are a marvellous source of thought-provoking material as for instance: 'An atheist is one who has no invisible means of support.' And 'Is there life *before* death?'

Eden Philpotts: The Universe is full of magical things, patiently waiting for our wits to grow sharp.

Ralph Cudworth: Truth and Love are two of the most powerful things in the world; and when they both go together they cannot be easily withstood.

Henri Frédéric Amiel: Tell me what you feel in your room when the full moon is shining in upon you and your lamp is dying out, and I will tell you how old you are, and I shall know if you are happy.

Henry Thoreau, again: If a man does not keep pace with his companions, perhaps it is because he hears a different drummer. Let him step to the music which he hears, however measured or far away.

Mark Twain: All you need in this life is ignorance and confidence, and then success is sure.

Two lines from a poem by Andrew Marvell have haunted me for years. The poem is called 'The Garden'. I have never read it in its entirety, but once, years ago, discovered the two lines in a book of quotations, and remembered them. The picture those words put into my mind will probably be entirely different from the picture you see. All I know is they have always had the strangest, most beautiful effect on me. I hope they do with you. The lines are these:

> *Annihilating all that's made*
> *To a green thought in a green shade.*

I'm not sure I would want to read the rest of the poem, even if I were to find it. The impression created would be subtly altered. Those lines are sufficient for me, as were the first two lines of Meredith's poem, 'The Woods of Westermain', written in 1883:

> *Enter these enchanted woods,*
> *You who dare.*

I found that poem, read it, and it did nothing for me. Yet those first lines are as haunting as those in Marvell's poem. Such images are conjured up by them that go far beyond the words. All these bits and pieces have gone into my scrapbook, and more, like this, from Nelson Boswell: 'If you can keep your head while those about you are losing theirs, perhaps you do not understand the situation.'

I write poems down as well if they particularly appeal to me. John Donne has written some of the most beautiful love poems, as has Shakespeare. The following are two of my favourites. The first, John Donne's 'The Anniversarie':

All other things, to their destruction draw,
Only our love hath no decay;
This, no tomorrow hath, nor yesterday,
Running it never runs from us away,
But truly keepes his first, last, everlasting day.

And William Shakespeare's Sonnet 109:

As easy might I from myself depart,
As from my soul, which in thy breast doth lie:
That is my home of love; if I have rang'd,
Like him that travels, I return again.

The Queen read a piece of poetry on one of her Christmas broadcasts that had been sent to her by someone unknown:

When all your world is torn with grief and strife,
Think yet — when there seems nothing left to mend
The frail and time-worn fabric of your life,
The golden thread of courage has no end.

And the following, 'The Salutation to the Dawn', from the Sanskrit:

Look to this day
For it is the very life of life
In its brief course lie all the varieties and realities of your existence:
The glory of action,
The bliss of growth,
The splendour of beauty,
For yesterday is but a dream and tomorrow is only a vision;
But today well lived makes every yesterday a dream of happiness
*   and every tomorrow a vision of hope.*
Look well, therefore, to this day.

All these have given me pleasure and just as important as that, something else; inspiration. Another poem of John Donne's, 'The Good Morrow', gave me the title for a book. The last two lines of the first verse are:

If ever any beauty I did see,
Which I desir'd and got, t'was but a dreame of thee.

A Dream of Thee came about simply because of reading that poem, and it is one I enjoyed writing very much.

Quotations and poems are wonderful things to collect in a scrapbook. Equally so are the incidents, humorous and otherwise, that happen in all our lives, those things that enrich our world for us. For instance, travelling by road can be a pleasure for any writer. Do you visualise the same giant geranium lurching from one side of the road to the other whenever you see the sign 'HEAVY PLANT CROSSING'? Do you know what a Dangerou is? You don't? I see it as a large Australian animal, a mixture between a dingo and a kangeroo. I'm not sure why it bends, as indicated on the sign 'DANGEROUS BEND' but when we turn the rather sharp curve we are approaching, we may find out. And oh, to have been in the car with those American tourists recently as they drove through our glorious English countryside. 'Gee, Elmer,' the wife exclaimed, 'don't these English villages have the quaintest names?' And her husband, reading out loud the sign 'SLOW, LOOSE CHIPPINGS AHEAD', was forced to agree!

I discovered only recently – to my shame – that the word I had known all my life as mizzled, as in 'I have been mizzled', was in fact pronounced mis-led. That aurie – as in 'things have gone sadly aurie' – was actually said as a-wry. I knew it was *spelt* awry. I just never knew how to say it. And when in childhood days I read in the papers that a man had been sent to gaol for a year, I used to wonder what football team he played for.

My mental scrapbook is also full of incidents, experiences, people, places – everything in fact. I wonder if every other writer enjoys this same rich store of material? I'm sure they do. Before I venture into a new book I dip into my memory store to see if there is anything I can use.

I have walked down a Paris street at four in the morning when the world was almost asleep and there was no traffic, and I will remember that as long as I live. I walked through Paris streets at night four years ago, yet it is the thirty-year-old memory that stays with me more vividly, etched for ever in my mind. Why? I don't know. Perhaps because I was eighteen and in love? Elizabeth Bowen wrote, 'Remote memories, already distorted by the imagination are more useful for the purposes of scene.

Unfamiliar, or once-seen places yield more than do familiar, often-seen places.'

I have sat in the courtyard of a French château used as a youth hostel, eating ham and black olives with bread. That also was thirty years ago, but I remember the taste of the ham and olives and the bitter sharpness of the cheap red wine we were drinking. I can still see the necklace of lights strung out like diamonds along the front at Cannes across the sea from the hostel, and the moon overhead reflected in the water. The fragrance of eucalyptus stays with me still, as does the memory of the open-air dance floor with a canopy of vines overhead and the chirrup of the cicadas. All these are still so clear to me that it is almost as though I can reach out and touch them even now. And walking over rocky paths in rope-soled espadrilles and swimming in the warm Mediterranean.

Memory plays tricks, as Elizabeth Bowen said. Some things are blurred but in these memories is the reflection of the girl I was and how I felt as I saw these things, never dreaming then that they would remain with me for ever, and somehow, something of this comes over when I am writing, an echo from the past. We all have our recollections of such golden days when the world was a wonderful place waiting to be explored, when we knew it all, so much more than those older and wiser. Treasure those remembrances because when you are writing about your eighteen-year-old heroines you will know how she feels. You will, for a brief time, be eighteen again.

And that is the end of my scrapbook. It's back to work again ...

SEVENTEEN

The Vatman Cometh

WHEN you achieve modest financial success after having your first book accepted, you will find that certain gentlemen become very interested in you, and when you go on to make larger amounts of money then some other gentlemen will also express great concern. I am not referring, alas, to divine-looking six-foot-four hunks of virile manhood with dark hair and steely grey eyes, but to those gentlemen who work respectively for Her Majesty's Inland Revenue and Her Majesty's Customs & Excise departments.

The first piece of advice in this section is that you obtain for yourself the services of a good accountant as soon as your first book starts making you money. When your income is modest his advice will be valuable, and when you go on to make a great deal of money it will be essential. More than that: he will actually be able to understand those almost incomprehensible forms which arrive from time to time, causing palpitations in the heart of every honest citizen. Most writers are not numerate; all accountants are, or they wouldn't be accountants. I cherish mine, and give him cups of tea and biscuits when he comes to see me, and even on occasion a glass of wine (but only after he's finished fiddling with his calculator and totting up all the sums of money I have to pay).

You may be as surprised as I was to find out exactly what you can claim as legitimate expenses. Herewith a list:

1 All stationery. This includes of course, the minutiae of a

writer's study: paperclips, rubber bands, stapling machine, notepads, gummed labels, Tipp-ex, etc., as well as the more obvious items like typing paper, carbons, exercise books and ring binders.

2 Postage, and packaging, including envelopes, sellotape and/or sealing wax.

3 Telephone and answering machine.

4 Accountancy fees and (if you have one) agent's fees.

5 Subscriptions to periodicals and magazines, and newspapers (if you use these for research purposes).

6 Visits to theatres or cinemas for research purposes.

7 The cost of typewriting or secretarial help.

8 A proportion of the heating, lighting, cleaning costs and rates of the rooms of work in your home. Do not classify one room as your sole place of work, it could result in you having to pay Capital Gains Tax if you move house. It is better to use two rooms or more and spread out the expense accordingly.

9 Reference books and replacing same.

10 The cost of annual overhaul of typewriter, and any repairs, of course.

11 Travelling and hotel costs for research purposes.

12 Car expenses (petrol, tax, maintenance) if it is used for research purposes.

Regarding typewriters, word processors, video machines and similar items that may be essential to your writing and research, you would be well advised to talk this over with your accountant as there is something called Capital Allowances which I do not fully understand (this is where I start to get a headache) but he does.

Obviously there are lots of other things that I may not have thought of, but you might. The first time I was asked to be on television I bought a new outfit and had my hair done at a very expensive hairdresser. Always game for a laugh, I asked Gary, my accountant, if I would be able to claim for these, expecting a 'no' I must admit, and he said, 'We can but try', and we did, and lo, they were allowed. You have nothing to lose by asking, you see.

It is also advisable to be guided by your accountant in the matter of separate taxation from your spouse if he too is earning a decent salary. This is called 'electing for separate assessment'. You will then both be taxed as single people and keep more of your respective salaries than if it were lumped together as one income. This is, of course, after a while, when you are earning quite a lot of money, which leads me on to the next subject and the heading of this chapter, 'The Vatman Cometh'.

VAT, or Value Added Tax to give it its correct title, is payable by all writers whose annual income exceeds £18,700. (This is the figure at the time of writing, but it may be altered from time to time. The simplest way to find out is to telephone your local VAT office.) When you have been writing for a few years, and see your royalties creeping closer and closer to that magic number, contact your local VAT office and tell them so. You'll find it under Customs & Excise in the telephone directory. They will send you a form to register and you will then have a certificate with your very own number on. Isn't that nice! It doesn't matter if you sign on before you earn that amount; in fact it is better to do it before rather than after. I *speak from experience*. It is only when you have received a letter from Customs & Excise threatening you with prosecution that you can fully know the meaning of the words dread and horror. I was an innocent creature ten years ago and my first accountant had just retired and somehow things got forgotten in the changeover. I had quite a lot of backdated VAT to pay, and difficulties in claiming it back. It is an advantage to be VAT-registered because not only will your publisher pay it for you but you can claim the VAT back on all you pay for items connected with your work. To do this it is necessary to obtain VAT invoices whenever you buy stationery, or anything else subject to VAT, to do with your writing. The only headache is the quarterly forms you have to fill in, but your accountant will do those for you. All you have to do is sign, and write the cheque out.

In order for your publisher to reimburse you the VAT on your royalties, you will need to invoice him, and for this purpose I bought a Collins Invoice Duplicate book. For entering all my VAT-rated purchases (or inputs as HM Customs & Excise quaintly calls them) I bought a Collins Cathedral Analysis book.

I don't have shares in Collins, honestly, and I dare say any good stationer's would have many similarly efficient books, but these are fine for me. Margery Hilton, a very popular Mills & Boon writer, advised me to get these books and then kindly showed me how to enter everything correctly, and because I think visual aids are always easier to understand than written explanations, I am reproducing a typical page from each book below. First the invoice book, then the one for VAT.

INVOICE				Date:		
From: Polly Purplehearts, The Rose Bower, Hitchin, Herts. To: Messrs Bills & Coos, 25 Cliffhanger Lane, London W99				*VAT reg. no.* 150.9999.12		
				Type of Supply Book		
Date of Supply	Description	Amount Exluding VAT		VAT Rate	VAT Amount	
30.6.86	Advance on Royalties (*Passion's flames*)	2000	00	15%	300	00
	Total	2000	00			
	Add VAT Amount	300	00			
	Total payable inc. VAT	2300	00			

OUTPUTS (Royalties)   Page 1

| | | | A | B | C |
Date	Description	Inv. No.	Royalties & Advances	VAT	Total
13.6.85	Advance on *Love in a Mist*	1	2,000.00	300.00	2,300.00

INPUTS (Purchases)   Page 2

| | | | D | E | F | G |
Date	Supplier	Inv. No.	Total	Goods	VAT	Non-deductible VAT
20.6.85	W.H. Smith (stationery)	1	28.50	24.23	4.27	
21.6.85	Accountant's fee	2	34.50	30.00	4.50	

First an explanation of the letters A-B-C etc. which I have
inserted above certain columns. I did this for my own benefit
when I used to fill in my own VAT forms from Customs and
Excise. First, I made a copy of their VAT form, stuck it inside the
front cover of my invoice book, and put those letters at the side
of the little boxes you have to fill in. For instance: the line on the
VAT form which says: 'TAX due on OUTPUTS' has my letter
B beside it so that I know that I enter my VAT column figures in
it (£300.00); another line on their form says 'Total Tax
Deductible' beside that I have written F so that I know the VAT
on my purchases goes in there (£8.77). With me so far? If not,

you need an accountant even more than I do. No, I don't know why royalties are called 'outputs', and purchases you make are called 'inputs', but that is what HM C. & E. in their wisdom, call them. You just have to go along with it. I wish you the best of luck. When you first register for VAT you will be assigned your very own VAT man, who is not the terrifying figure that we have been led to believe from the various horror stories in newspapers. He is a civil servant with a job to do. He is always available by telephone if you have queries, and will come and see you in your home at approximately two-year intervals to inspect your books. Treat him like a human being and you'll be pleasantly surprised at how helpful he can be.

And now for something completely different: PLR, which stands for Public Lending Right, and means quite simply that you will earn money each time one of your books is borrowed from a public library. The first requirement for registration is that you should have had a book published. The second is that you should write to: The Public Lending Right Office, Bayheath House, Prince Regent Street, Stockton-on-Tees, Cleveland TS18 1DF (Telephone: 0642-604699).

They will send you a form on which you will enter your book (or books) in a list. Enter both hardback and paperback editions, plus large-print editions (if any), plus, in every case, the ISBN. This is usually to be found on the back cover and also on the copyright page. It means International Standard Book Number, and is unique to your book. When you have entered all these, it is necessary for you to have the form, and your signature upon it, witnessed and signed by a solicitor. Then you send everything off to the above address and wait for the money to come in. What could be nicer? I'm now making extra money on the books I wrote twelve years ago.

The PLR is calculated on borrowings from a sample twenty public libraries; a payment of about a penny per borrowing per book is paid, and the figures multiplied in proportion to total library lending to produce, for each book, an estimate of its total annual loans throughout Great Britain. For an example, one of my earlier books, *Laird of Gaela*, was borrowed 33,826 times, thus bringing me in £292.67. Another, *Law of the Jungle*, was taken out 48,828 times – money earned £422.48. Some books were taken out in only small numbers, a couple of hundred times or less, thus earning only a few pounds *but* – and this is important – even if you have only two or three books published and they are in the libraries they have the potential to earn you several hundred pounds, which is why it is sensible to register immediately your first book is published. Books published and registered before 30 June will attract all the loans reported for the previous twelve months, as July to June is the PLR year. You will of course have to pay income tax on your PLR earnings, but not VAT. And that's it. It wasn't too painful, was it?

And finally ...

AND finally, a brief word to the total beginner. Yes to you. You who have never, ever written anything before – yes, I know you always received the highest marks for English Composition in school, and all your friends say you write the most interesting letters and postcards, but that doesn't count any more. You are about to write your very first book.

Congratulations! You are embarking on the most exciting journey you will ever make in your life. There is nothing to beat the feeling you'll have as you write 'Chapter One' in bold black letters on virgin paper. Except perhaps the one you'll experience when at last, after many trials and tribulations, laughter and tears and perhaps a journey that spans the globe, you write 'The End', after 55,000 exciting words. 55,000! That's a lot of words. I know, I know. And between page one, Chapter One, and that final page there will be countless thousands of letters all jumbled up to form those words, comprising your toil, perspiration and, oh yes, imagination.

That journey may take you as little as a month or as long as a year. You may write the book with such joy that you'll wonder why you didn't try it years ago, or it may be a gargantuan effort that leaves you reeling with exhaustion. But you will have *done* it. You. All by yourself. Created a world full of people who are unique to you. Isn't that a wonderful feeling? You're a writer.

If you want to write, don't let anyone or anything stop you. If you are really determined, nothing will be allowed to anyway. If you are half-hearted about it, distractions will abound, leaping out at you from all sorts of unlikely places, as tempting as that first apple in the Garden of Eden. It is your choice. You'll have off-days when nothing seems to go right, and to balance those there will be days of such wonder and delight that words flow faster than you can keep up with, and you'll have to scribble down exquisite gems that well up from your subconscious onto separate pieces of paper so that you won't forget them as you concentrate on what you are doing at *that* moment. There will be other times when you feel as though you are trying to walk through a field of treacle, progress extremely slow and a great effort. All these things have happened to every writer at some time, excitement and frustration mingling until we're tempted to fling the manuscript to the corner of the room. It's normal. It's part of being a writer.

You will find that when inspiration is flowing, you can write under the most adverse conditions and scarcely notice. I've written on one Christmas Day morning at 7 o'clock, with toys scattered round the tree, the sound of trumpets and drums coming from another part of the house, the room cold because the heating hadn't come on, in the kitchen a turkey waiting to be stuffed, me clad in nightie and dressing gown, and with a throbbing head from a mixture of incipient flu and one glass too many of sherry at the previous evening's next-door neighbours' party. Why? Because the words were bursting to be let out and I simply couldn't stop them, so I wrote, and finished the chapter and only then could I go and do the thousand other tasks that needed doing.

I wrote a book called *The Benedict Man* during the time of the power-cuts, when every household in Great Britain was zoned. We were Zone E, I remember, and when it was our turn, all the power was cut off on certain evenings between 6 and 10 p.m. It was great fun for the children, who looked forward to cooking baked beans and sausages on an open fire. But I was then typing *The Benedict Man* and I wanted to post it, and I didn't care about baked beans and sausages or smoky cups of tea, I minded very much that it was almost impossible to see without the aid of candles – which, in case you didn't know are not the best things to see typewriter keys by – and I worked with two candles, one either side of the machine, until I could see no longer, so then I took a pencil torch, stuck it in my mouth and typed until the lights came on. Yes, I had aching front teeth as well as sore eyes – but I posted the typescript off the next morning. Was it worth it? Yes. Would I do it again? Yes, if I had to. I'd decided that nothing was going to stop me – and it didn't. So please, don't let anything stop you. You will find out why for yourself. Good luck, new writer.

A Postscript for the Paperback ...

At the end of the hardback edition of this book, which came out in August 1985, I set a simple competition. One hundred pounds for one hundred words. Readers could send in either the first 100 words of a romantic novel, or describe, again in 100 words, the first encounter between hero and heroine. I expected a correspondingly simple response, say fifty or so entries. Ha!

The closing date for the competition was to be 30 June 1986, my birthday. When the first typescript arrived within a week of the book's publication, I was mildly surprised, and this was followed by several more over the next couple of weeks. I read them and put them away in a thin envelope-type holder. Within two months I had to buy a box file to hold the growing pile, and by January the box had become two. It was then that it began to dawn on me that perhaps my guess of fifty entries had been a slight underestimation! There came a mad rush in spring, when a young man's fancy, so it's said, lightly turns to thoughts of love, and both young men's and women's fancies lightly turn to thoughts of entering competitions (a goodly portion of these entries were from men). And now I had in my study *three* box files bursting with entries. By the time my birthday arrived the total of entries was 557. Four boxes full!

Several weeks before the closing date I had sat down and sorted through the stack of typescripts and put them into four piles of 'marvellous', 'very good', 'good', and 'hmm, well!', to ease my load of work for when the time came for the final selection. Most of the entries were accompanied by letters and/or birthday cards. (I received more cards on my birthday than I'd ever had in my life, around sixty!) And all the letters were very flattering, as were all the other letters that were arriving around the same time, without competition entries. I was in grave danger of getting an extremely swollen head by this time. I did have fun reading them, and my typist was fully engaged for several days, helping me to reply to them all. Many of these fan letters were extremely witty, many were poignant, telling of solitary writing struggles over the years. Some of those were very moving. It seems I had tapped a well when I wrote *To Writers With Love*, because so many of my correspondents wrote: 'I thought I was all alone in my struggles, but your book has given me confidence to go on.' One woman assured me that she had been about to throw herself in the nearest river in her despair at not being accepted, and the book had arrived in the nick of time and saved her life! As the rest of the letter was exceedingly funny, I assumed poetic licence on her part. Dramatic, but not exactly true. I suspect she'll make a good romantic novelist.

The publicity that accompanied the launch of the book was fantastic. Buchan & Enright introduced me to Beth Macdougall, who took me to lunch, said, 'Leave it all to me', and shortly afterwards produced a comprehensive schedule of television, radio, and newspaper interviews. I'd never met a walking dynamo before, but that's what she is. We also had a load of laughs, in between dodging round London in taxis over the next few weeks. In fact, I spent so much time commuting there for various interviews that family and animals were puzzled by the stranger who appeared every so often and said: 'Hello, I'm home again.'

Peter Grosvenor of the *Daily Express* telephoned to ask if he could come up to Manchester to interview me, which I found quite flattering. It emerged that he was a cricket fanatic, and there just happened to be a match on at Old Trafford against the Australians that day. (I live about six miles away.) That *was* a coincidence, wasn't it! The interview was fun, though, and when, after an entertaining evening, Derek and I ran Peter to his hotel in the centre of Manchester and went in for a drink with him, and discovered that the entire Australian team were staying there, and mingling with us at the bar, Peter's cup of happiness ran over. He gave the book a very pleasant write-up. Well, he had to after that, didn't he?

Gillian Fairchild, Features Editor of *Good Housekeeping*, entertained me right royally at the Ritz and wrote a super article. All the reviews, over thirty, were a pleasure to read, although I was savaged by Kenneth Robinson on *Start The Week* on Radio 4. It was nothing personal, I was assured by friends. He did it to everybody. Reports that I was seen rolling round the floor clutching my sides and laughing when I read a few months later that he'd got the sack and was 'very upset' about it are just not true. I prefer to laugh standing up. A breakfast television interview on BBC with Janet Brown and Nick Ross was much more fun. Her witty autobiography, *Prime Mimicker* was due out shortly afterwards, and we have signed copies of each other's books. A lovely lady.

Enough of all this publicity, except for one little gem I must share. I was awarded the first, and only, 'Black Hole Award' by the Crime Writers' Association. When they sent me the review about it, it read: 'Anyone who reads *To Writers with Love* and doesn't go on to write a best-seller deserves to be cast into the outermost Black Hole.' I dusted a place on the sideboard specially for the award, but I suspect that it must have swallowed itself up en route. I'll never know.

Now to the entries themselves. It was no easy task to pick a winner, I can tell you. Sorting through the hundreds of entries to find the best was the hardest work I have ever done. The four piles were read several times, not only by me but by writer friends I had begged or bribed to help. A few entries – very few – were moved from one pile to another, after due deliberation. But in essence they remained the same, and at the end of many hours' hard slog I was left with a stack of about seventy typescripts from which I knew the winner would emerge.

Many late nights, cups of coffee, biscuits and a handy bottle of aspirins followed. Many times did I curse whoever had planted the idea of such a simple competition in my head. And many times did I swear softly at myself for doing it. I didn't want there to be any losers. What's more, at least 300 of the entries were accompanied by stamped addressed envelopes for the return of the manuscripts – and most of them had the earnest entreaty: 'Please say a few words of criticism, even if I don't win.' So I tried to oblige, and that too was hard work.

Slowly but surely, the seventy were whittled down to twenty-five. I must digress for a moment and tell you where some of these entries came from. Apart from the obvious major section coming from all parts of the UK, there were many from the United States, Canada, Australia, Eire, then — wait for it — entries from the following, some very far-flung, locations: Holland, France, Spain, Japan, Luxemburg, Papua New Guinea, South Africa, Germany; in the main written by British women living in those places. My mother had a field day with all the exotic stamps (she collects them for various charities), while I spent hours at various post offices counting out international reply coupons!

Several things emerged from this tonnage of words. The majority of the entrants had taken time and care to send in impeccable entries. Correct spelling, excellent typing, length *exactly* one hundred words. They were a pleasure to read. *Some were not*. There were spelling mistakes, Tippex blobs, and grammatical errors galore — and all *that* in 100 words! Some people had sent me 300 words or more (perhaps they couldn't count), and a few had sent multiple entries and asked me to choose the best. Some had sent entries that bore no relation to the beginning of a romantic novel or of any other kind of novel I have ever read.

I marvelled at the difference in attitude. If I decided to enter a competition, and one of the rules was that I send in exactly 100 words, then that is what I would send in. And I would make sure that my entry was neat. Did they think I wouldn't *notice*? I did. And every other judge of every other competition that is ever set also notices when rules are broken, or bent, or mislaid. And, surely, to obey simple rules (and they couldn't have been simpler in my case) is the beginning of a professional attitude. And without that, no one can hope to succeed in a competitive market.

I have had the pleasure of meeting some of my finalists, at various writers' conferences, over the past year, and was able to tell them how delighted I was with their entries; and, without exception, I was impressed by their professional attitude to their work. I'm quite sure that I'll be hearing from some of them soon, when their first books are accepted. There were, inevitably, several beautifully typed and presented entries that did not come within the semi-final seventy. They'd obeyed the rules but the content was just not right, either by virtue of being too slow-moving or totally different from what I had specified. The argument could be made that it is extremely difficult to write anything vivid and meaningful in 100 words. I have two answers to this. One: that was the whole point of the challenge; it was designed to get the very best effort from the minds of those taking it up. And, two: read the book of *Sunday Telegraph* Mini Sagas. That is full of excellent *complete stories in fifty words*. But as I say, so many of the entrants succeeded beautifully. Their work was a pleasure to read, encapsulating an atmosphere of a book to follow that would be a delight. And I wanted to know what might happen next.

I'm going to show you the three eventual winners – two joint firsts and a third, together with my comments. Now, because my daughter didn't win the Miss Pear's contest when she was four, I know exactly how some of you entrants will feel when you read the three prize-winning entries. You will be as cross as I was when Judith failed to come first when she was clearly the most beautiful child out of thousands of entrants. You'll know, as I did, that your 'baby' would have been the best! Anyone who adjudicates any kind of contest tries to be as objective as possible, but we're all human, and choice is a very personal thing. I only know that, in the end, these were the ones that had most consistently appealed to me; and, yes, if I could have awarded seventy prizes, I would have done so, because there were some really superb entries among that final number and it was extremely difficult to make the final decision.

Joint First Prize: Bet Medcalf, of Staffordshire

Suddenly an arm encircled her waist and lifted her into the building. After the glare of the street all she could see was that he was big.

'What the hell do you think you are doing?' she shouted furiously.

'Probably saving your life,' he replied.

'Good God, I'm a professional photographer. I know the risks.'

'O.K., get yourself killed. Pity to lose a good camera though.' He grabbed the Hasselblad and held it high – a good foot beyond her reach. She hit him with all her nine stones. It was like punching a garden shed.

Then the car bomb exploded.

Background and atmosphere are conveyed here with great skill. Heroine clearly a fiercely independent woman, and the hero is big, quick-thinking, and tough, which is precisely what the readers (and me!) love best. There is humour too, when she hits him – 'like punching a garden shed' – which adds to the terrific impact of that last line. To capture all that in 100 words left me open-mouthed with admiration.

Joint First Prize: Kathryn Waugh, of London

The envelope was addressed to her, Jane Morrison, and bore stamps from Barbados but Jane did not know anyone who lived in the West Indies.

She withdrew a large photograph and looked into the face of a man she had never seen before. On the back was written: 'To Jane, with love – the girl I intend to marry.' It was signed 'Adam'. There was no letter, just the picture.

Flushed and angry she took the envelope marked 'Photographs, do not bend.' 'Oh, don't they?' Jane mused as she prepared to tear it up. Then she looked at the face again ...

This appealed to me the day it arrived. Simply written, with a lovely touch of humour in the final paragraph, and a touch of mystery in the preceding two, it is delightful, and surely the perfect beginning of a romantic novel. So many questions asked, which we can be sure will be answered in the book. Who *is* he? And how does he know her, when she has never heard of *him*? And can we look forward to clashes ahead? You bet we can!

Runner-up: Vera Vavasour of Bournemouth

'The thirteenth rejection,' Mimsy surveyed the parcel in despair. 'I give up.' She tossed the manuscript from the fourth-floor window. 'I have wasted my life.'

Rock Stern's brown eyes noticed the heavy envelope in

time. He dodged, but was not prepared for what followed. Some of the 'How to Write a Novel' books were paperback, but Bainton's 1890 *Art of Authorship* felled him and the descent of both volumes of the *Compact OED* drew much blood.

'You've probably killed him,' Felicia leaned out her dark head.

'Good. Pity they can't hang me for it,' the tearful slim blonde declared.

This is simply hilarious, and very promising. I laughed out when I read it, as did the friends I showed it to. I wanted to know why Mimsy had had thirteen rejections (she'd obviously not read *To Writers With Love*) and if she ran down to help the stricken Rock Stern afterwards. Very enjoyable.

Incidentally, the joint winners of the first prize both turned out to be men, writing under women's pseudonyms – which caused a certain amount of happy confusion at first.

Well, now you've read the winners, and the comments. The competition generated so many lovely side-effects, for want of a better expression. I have introduced entrants to other entrants – by post of course – and, for all I know, they've started flourishing writer's groups; the Romantic Novelists' Association has been inundated with enquiries as to how to join, and Scarborough Writers Weekend was also flooded with applications.

Thanks to everyone who cut out that little coupon in the back of the hardback edition, and took the trouble to send an entry. It was hard work, but it was great fun while it lasted.

So now, get writing your book, all of you, and one day when you've had several published, and decide to write a book telling others how to do it, and you decide to have a competition, take my advice – buy several large box files. You'll need 'em! Good luck.

Index

Page numbers of main entries are printed in **bold** type